"So you admit we had chemistry."

"Have. Have chemistry."

The temperature rose another degree. Joanna closed the gap along the couch and ran her fingers over his hand.

"What are you telling me?" Cooper's voice had gone a little rough.

"I think you know."

"And I think you know it's not going to happen as long as we're working together."

Now he chose to be honorable? Honestly. Men.

"We're not working right now."

"You're splitting hairs." But even as he spoke, his gaze dropped to her collarbone, to her chest....

The fact that she wasn't wearing a bra seemed to detonate in his head.

"You're not playing fair," he whispered.

She had him.

Blaze™

Dear Reader,

People always ask me where I get my ideas. Well, the idea for *No Rules* came as I walked past a newsstand and saw a headline that said, "Succumb Here Often?" Which, of course, is guaranteed to grab the attention of a Harlequin Blaze writer! The article was about ways, new and old, that men use to communicate with women when they're trying to get together.

My brain went to work right away, and since Cooper Maxwell, one of my investigators in my fictional California Law Enforcement Unit, had been demanding his own story for some time, I gave in. But what he didn't know was that he'd be paired with a woman who not only has issues with authority—she's the hottest thing he's ever seen. I hope you enjoy their story, as well as peeks at what happened to Linn and Kellan from *His Hot Number*, and Tessa and Griffin from *Sex & Sensibility*.

I love to hear from readers. Stop by my Web site, www.shannonhollis.com, and drop me a line!

Warmly,

Shannon Hollis

NO RULES
Shannon Hollis

HARLEQUIN®

TORONTO • NEW YORK • LONDON
AMSTERDAM • PARIS • SYDNEY • HAMBURG
STOCKHOLM • ATHENS • TOKYO • MILAN • MADRID
PRAGUE • WARSAW • BUDAPEST • AUCKLAND

ISBN-13: 978-0-373-79335-8
ISBN-10:   0-373-79335-9

NO RULES

This is a work of fiction. Names, characters, places and incidents are
either the product of the author's imagination or are used fictitiously,
and any resemblance to actual persons, living or dead, business
establishments, events or locales is entirely coincidental.

This edition published by arrangement with Harlequin Books S.A.

® and TM are trademarks of the publisher. Trademarks indicated with
® are registered in the United States Patent and Trademark Office, the
Canadian Trade Marks Office and in other countries.

www.eHarlequin.com

Printed in U.S.A.

Books by Shannon Hollis

HARLEQUIN BLAZE
144—HIS HOT NUMBER
170—ON THE LOOSE
203—SEX & SENSIBILITY
254—FULL CIRCLE

For Karen, Anne, Ellen, Mary Kay, Cathy
and Maddie with thanks for thuds, wild spins
and unstinting support

1

First Rule: Attraction is the first phase of the biological imperative to procreate. It is not an involuntary response.

Club Atlantis
Santa Rita, California
22:27 hours

"DEEP DOWN, every woman wants to be seduced."

The words of his instructor echoed in his head like a mantra as Marvin Musselmann zeroed in on the brunette sitting alone at the table farthest from the dance floor. A sparkly, beaded handbag on the Plexiglas stool next to her told him she had a companion. A female companion.

He glanced at Cody Zimmer, fellow student of the Rules, who was his wingman. "It's not going to work."

Even if he got her phone number, he wasn't carrying any pens in the pocket of his new dress shirt. What was he going to write with? He could remember thousands of bytes of software code, but when it came to a woman's phone number, it erased itself from his memory faster than a virus could take out a hard drive.

"It will work." It was Cody's job to spot him the way a trainer would spot a beginning athlete. "You know what to do. You just have to execute."

"I can't."

"You only have to do it once," Cody assured him for the seventh time. No, eighth. The seventh had been in the car, just before the valet had taken his keys.

No keys, no pen. Marvin felt naked.

"Now, go on. By the time her friend comes back, you'll have scored and you can spot me."

"Okay. Okay." Marvin shook out his hands as if he were going to belly up to a video game, and blew out a few breaths to increase the oxygen in his blood.

Game face.

And for God's sake, don't forget the Rules.

The woman looked up as he approached. Before that bored, "oh, no, not another loser" look seeped into her eyes and unmanned him, he smiled. His instructor had told him he had a good smile. He'd bought new clothes, since the gabardine trousers and 1976 Grateful Dead T-shirt he habitually wore to work at Applied Infographics were not, he had been informed, appropriate in a social situation.

The smile and the clothes, so far, had staved off that look he dreaded.

"You have beautiful eyes—I was admiring them from over there." His mouth was dry, so he swallowed and moistened his lips. "Do you mind if I sit down until your friend comes back?"

She shrugged, and relief flooded him. As he sat, he touched her wrist. "I hardly ever go downtown anymore, but I'm glad I did tonight."

Now her gaze was definitely interested. His fingers slid under her wrist to the pulse point, and his heart rate picked up. The moment of truth. He would either have to beat feet back to Cody and drown his humiliation in alcohol, or he'd clinch a companion for the night. He had two condoms in his wallet and enough money for a nice hotel room.

But no pen for her phone number.

Stop. Focus, he told himself. Don't lose your nerve.

"They call this place Atlantis because it's supposed to look like we're underwater. I like all these undulating lines and the clear furniture." The woman leaned toward him, her gaze locked on his mouth. He forced himself to keep talking as he stroked her wrist with his forefinger. "And the way people are spread out over three floors, enjoying themselves. I really like that."

Her lips parted. "Me, too," she said. Was that a breathless note in her voice?

My God, he thought. This really works.

"Celie, who's this?"

The sharp voice over his left shoulder made Marvin turn, startled. A blonde with a swimmer's smooth muscles picked up the beaded handbag he'd moved to the third chair at the table, caution and surprise in her eyes.

His fingers never breaking their electric connection with the brunette's skin, he said, "I'm Marvin. Celie and I were getting to know one another."

"He's my date," the brunette said dreamily. Her eyes never left his face.

"I thought *I* was your date." The blonde dropped into the third chair. "Honestly, I take two seconds to go to the ladies and you're—"

"Marv, buddy, I thought I'd find you down here." Cody touched the back of the blonde's neck as he slid into the fourth chair, and she blinked. "Why don't you introduce me to these beautiful ladies?"

Marvin did—well, the blonde introduced herself when Cody put out his hand for a handshake.

And Marvin watched the Rules work their magic a second time.

It was a miracle, especially for a guy who hadn't had a date since his dissertation was completed. Surreptitiously, he patted his back pocket. Wallet, money and condoms. Still there.

Sex. The final frontier.

Marvin could hardly wait.

2

Carmel, California
17:35 hours

COOPER MAXWELL, Investigator Level II, member of the elite California Law Enforcement Unit whose personnel were handpicked from every police department in the state, hunched his shoulders under his tuxedo jacket and considered the horror of the situation before him.

"We don't really have to dance." He appealed to Danny Kowalski, narcotics specialist, who was standing next to him in a penguin suit just like his, cummerbund and all.

"If I have to dance, you have to dance," Danny said flatly. "Don't even try to fake a phone call and weasel out of it. At least you get the maid of honor—Linn's sister is a nice kid. I get the third cousin or whoever she is, and all I know about her is that she's available. Which I've heard at least fifty times from as many different people."

"We are dead meat, you know that." Cooper's tone reflected his sense of impending doom. "Once you dance with them, they've got you wrapped up for the rest of the evening. And even as big as this place is, there's no escape."

The two of them returned to their surveillance of the wedding reception. The lawns of software mogul Jay Singleton's Carmel, California, estate stretched down to his private strip of beach. White tents flapped in the gentle breeze, while tables loaded with hors d'oeuvres filled the space between two open bars. Behind them, on the patio, Kellan Black and his new bride, Linn Nichols, were in the process of cutting the cake. Cooper just had time to open his mouth to shout a warning when Linn mashed carrot cake with cream cheese frosting all over her beloved's innocently open mouth.

Good thing he knew Kell gave as good as he got. Linn better look out for her dress.

And he and Danny had better look out for predators disguised as bridesmaids in strapless plum silk. He didn't object to the maid of honor, Linn's sister Tessa, in principle. She was at this moment blowing in the ear of a guy he understood to be Singleton's director of security. He'd heard a rumor that Tessa was psychic, but he found it hard to believe that a girl as blond and funny and, face it, sexy as Tessa Nichols could do stuff like locate people by touching something they'd once worn.

He sighed. He could go for blond and funny and sexy right now. But she was off-limits. Instead, there was the third cousin and several others like her, all with a thirtieth-birthday deadline and deadly purpose in their eyes. Was this some kind of massive matchmaking scheme? Could Linn really be that evil? What had he done to piss her off?

"Paranoia will destroy ya," he muttered under his breath, and looked around. Not even six o'clock and he was already on his third beer. He needed to get the next one cued up.

Shazam.

He blinked and elbowed Danny in the ribs. "Hey. Look over there."

Obediently, Danny suspended his triangulation of each bridesmaid's current position and looked over at the bar, where the bartender was handing over a glass of white wine.

"That's no third cousin."

Cooper hoped she was no relation of Linn's at all. The less family gossip that got back to his fellow investigator after her honeymoon, the better. If he had his way, he wouldn't be heading back to his hotel room alone tonight.

The woman took the glass and turned to speak to her companion, a no-nonsense brunette whom Cooper dismissed from the radar immediately. Instead, his gaze traveled in an appreciative line from the crown of her red hair, which was bobbed at the nape of a neck as graceful as a swan's, to the toes of her strappy, high-heeled sandals. In between, he spent several seconds at rest stops: on the curve of a pair of breasts that would make a sculptor weep, on a waist that only served to accentuate a derriere that was just a shade curvier than perfect, and—thank you, ocean breeze—on a pair of legs, bare of stockings, that went all the way to the top of the side slit of her floaty green dress.

"I think I'm in love."

"Congratulations," Danny said gruffly. "I think I'm going to commit suicide."

"And leave the third cousin in the lurch?"

"If this is the apex of my life and all I have to look forward to, yes."

"Cheer up. There's still beer. Good stuff, too. Singleton's no cheapskate. We need a trip to the bar. Now."

"Lead on."

Cooper sidled up next to the redhead and flashed his very best "I'm totally harmless and great in bed" grin. When the brunette caught his eye, he downgraded it to "I'm totally harmless," then turned to the bartender and ordered a couple of bottles of Sam Adams.

"Bride's side or groom's?" he asked the redhead when he and Danny were both armed with what they needed. Standard wedding question. The answer didn't mean a thing, but you could get away with asking anyone that and opening the conversation.

"Neither. I'm crashing."

Her tone was clipped and impatient when, from the look of her, he'd expected sultry and maybe Southern. As for the crashing part, that wasn't his business.

"Thank God. Someone has to improve the scenery around here."

Her gaze, as neutral as her gray eyes, rested on him for a second, then moved past him to the crowd. "Looks nice to me. I should be used to the ocean, but I'm not."

Was she a recent arrival from the Midwest? He tried to place an accent, but she didn't seem to have one. "I wasn't talking about the geography." He tried on another version of the killer grin.

"I was. Come on, Bella. At least we can get some food out of this."

She grabbed her friend by the elbow, turned on the ball of one slender foot and left him standing there.

O-o-kay.

Fortunately, he was not a man to give up easily, as any number of drug dealers and lowlifes could tell you. The lady was a stunner—and her left hand ringless. Both very good reasons to pursue all avenues of investigation with all possible speed.

"Would the bridal party please join the bride and groom on the dance floor?"

Down on the lawn, the emcee grinned as four grown men—Cooper and Danny included—attempted to impersonate flower arrangements.

"Come on, Coop." Tessa appeared at his elbow like a luscious little wood nymph. "This is the moment you've been waiting for. Griffin says he'll even take a picture of it for you."

"My heart overflows." He put a smile on for Tessa's sake and offered her his arm. "But if they play 'Three Times a Lady' I'm just going to go shoot myself."

"No service weapons allowed on the premises. Besides, I think Linn has it in writing that they won't."

The band launched into "Pride and Joy" instead, the Stevie Ray Vaughan standard Coop's brother-in-law had played for his bride when they'd been married six years ago. Fortunately, he'd allowed his sister to persuade him to take swing dance lessons before their wedding, and now a grand total of two of the steps came back to him. As he swung Tessa past him in a happy whirl of silk, he observed that that was two more than poor Danny knew. He was doing some kind of side-to-side thing with the third cousin that reminded him of a man pacing out his last steps to the gas chamber.

Of all the weekends in the world, couldn't some crime syndicate have picked this one to bring in a couple of tons of cocaine?

He acquitted himself pretty well, all things considered, and when Griffin came to get his lady and the portable dance floor filled with other guests, he went in search of the redhead for Round Two.

Aha.

She and the brunette—Billie? Berta?—had taken up a strategic position next to the dessert table, where Kellan had told him there was supposed to have been a chocolate fountain, but where there was now a large bowl of fruit and plates and plates of petits fours. The arrangements for the wedding had been one disaster after another. When an arson fire had charred the reception hall, Tessa had pulled some strings with Jay Singleton—he was still a little fuzzy on how she'd done it, but according to Kellan it had been payback for locating someone for the guy—and he had offered his sumptuous backyard for the event.

Coop was pleased for Linn that it had all worked out. The woman who had once coldcocked a drug importer with a bottle of Cabernet looked feminine and fragile in designer silk, and her eyes glowed with happiness as she circled the dance floor in Kellan's arms.

Coop felt pleased that he'd managed to survive the bridesmaids' dance. Just one more thing would make his day complete, and she was presently standing with her head tipped back as a bite of what looked like a marzipan-glazed tart slid down her throat.

"Oh, my God, that's good," she sighed in the brunette's direction as he came up behind her. "You've got to try one of those."

He'd like to try making that expression come to her face without the aid of confectionery. He'd bet his next paycheck he could do it, too. All he had to do was impress the sandals off her and get her to leave the reception with him. She was a crasher, after all. It wasn't like her future was invested in catching the bouquet.

The brunette nodded in Cooper's direction, and the redhead swung to face him.

"Any recommendations for me?" He nodded at the desserts, but his tone indicated he might be inquiring after her preference of sexual position. She could take it in whatever way she liked…but he'd bet a woman with a mouth like that would understand a hint when she heard one.

"I recommend you quit stalking me."

Or not.

"I'm not stalking you." He scrubbed his tone of any hint of innuendo. "I was hoping I could have this dance. My name's Cooper, by the way. Cooper Maxwell."

She inclined her head and didn't return the favor. "I don't think so, Mr. Maxwell."

"My friends call me Cooper."

"I am not your friend." A pause. "Mr. Maxwell."

Well, shit. A guy could only bang his head against a stone wall so many times before he got a headache.

He turned to go. "All right. No biggie. Enjoy your dess—"

"Oh, for God's sake, lighten up, Jo," the brunette said with a roll of her eyes. Bella, that was her name. "This is a party. Go dance and pretend you're having a good time."

Jo, huh? It suited her. Short and snappy, heavy on the snap.

"I'm not here to have a good time," Jo said. "I'm here because I have to be and you know it."

What kind of wedding crasher got forced into it?

"Can you forget that for two seconds and dance with the guy?"

"Uh, standing right here." Cooper waved. "That's okay. No problem. I was just leaving."

Jo sighed as if he'd just asked her to hand over the deed to her ranch in return for her mama's life. "Fine. One dance. Let's go."

Geesh. This ought to be fun.

The band slid into "Embraceable You" and she slid into his arms. One whole verse went by while he racked his brain trying to think of something to say that didn't include an apology for living.

"I'm sorry," she said at the beginning of the second refrain. "I'm cranky and I shouldn't have taken it out on you."

To his relief, her spine softened and she actually closed up the space between them from six inches to something that involved touching at chest and thigh. Now this was more like it.

"Anything I can do?"

She shook her head. "No. It's work related. Punishment detail. Working with a bunch of jerks possibly even jerkier than the ones I left at home. There's nothing anyone can do. I just have to grin and bear it."

He thought of asking her what in hell's half acre she did for a living, then decided not to. They still had part of a song left and hopes for later that evening were slowly resurrecting themselves. He wasn't about to do anything to jeopardize that. So he just gathered her closer and swayed with the music. Inch by cranky inch, she softened until her breasts were pushing gently at his chest and their thighs were brushing and touching, brushing and touching…

"Mmm." Her sigh was a throaty murmur in his ear. So she felt it, too. The music seemed to weave a sensual web around them, and far-off drumbeats of desire hinted at what they could be like together in a more private setting.

"You're a very good dancer," she said, eyes half closed.

Now was not the time to explain about his sister and the swing lessons. Now was the time to get things done.

"I'm good at a lot of things." His hand slid lower on her waist, down to her lumbar curve and that luscious peachy fanny.

A grip as merciless as a crab's claw stopped it just short of his goal. "Hold it right there."

Dazed with the clash between hope and reality, he couldn't quite compute why she was stepping back. But the look in those cold gray eyes cleared that up in a hurry.

"I said I'd give you a dance. Gropes aren't included."

"But I…but we…sorry…"

For the second time in twenty minutes, she turned on a dime and stalked away. This time he let her go, and, feeling flattened and a little foolish, wove through the crowd in search of Danny or someone else from the office he could vent to. Sheesh. What a cougar. No wonder she was having trouble with her coworkers, blowing hot and cold like that. Everyone was probably in a state of perpetual confusion, waiting for their heads to get bitten off.

"Maxwell. Over here."

Cooper suspended his angry musings and realized his lieutenant was under a stand of trees with a couple of other people, waving at him. He changed his trajectory and joined them.

His new boss of just a few weeks, Lieutenant Norgard, held the respect of his operators because of his loyalty to his teams. You never had to worry about being fed to the wolves with Norgard. If you gave him your best, he stood behind you. Period. Cooper had moved out of narcotics and into Crimes Against Persons after their spectacular takedown of Rick O'Reilly a few months before. It was the penultimate stop on the way to his career goal of Homicide. With a couple of nice arrests lately, he finally felt as though he was hitting his stride.

"Enjoying yourself?" the lieutenant inquired. He looked just as he did any day in the office, in a two-piece suit with a subdued tie. He could almost be on duty.

"Yes, sir." Cooper tugged at his crisp white collar. "I'll be glad when I can peel out of this thing, though."

"No doubt. Maxwell, I'd like you to meet Sergeant Isabella Waring, from the L.A. office. Bella, this is one of my newer recruits, out of the narcotics squad. Cooper Maxwell."

Cooper focused abruptly as the nondescript brunette walked up. The one who had just engineered his humiliation on the dance floor.

Sergeant? L.A. office? This woman was CLEU?

He stuck out his hand. "Nice to meet you." That was stupid. They'd already met. Maybe she'd keep that quiet.

She smiled at him, which rendered her face not quite so nondescript. "Investigator Maxwell."

Okay, so she knew how to keep her mouth shut. The next question was, how did she know the cougar?

"Bella and I need to brief you on your new assignment," Norgard went on. "We're going to team you up with one of her investigators on a new case. I figure that with your doctorate in psychology, you're just the guy I need to profile a predator, find him and get him off the streets."

Coop lifted his brows with interest. "A sexual predator? Operating locally?" He hadn't heard a thing about it. Then again, his turf was San Francisco, not the string of beach towns running down the coast, of which Santa Rita and Carmel were two.

"Yes, so we need to—" Sergeant Waring stopped herself and waved at someone behind Cooper. "Never mind. We can give you the full briefing in a few minutes. Here's my investigator now."

Cooper turned and found himself face-to-face with the cougar. Her eyes widened and she glanced from him to Sergeant Waring, accusation sparking in their depths. "Bella, what is this?"

"Thanks for joining us, Jo," the brunette said smoothly. "I'd like you to meet your new partner. Investigator Cooper Maxwell, this is Investigator Joanna MacPherson, Crimes Against Persons, Los Angeles Subdivision."

3

Carmel, California

PUNISHMENT DETAIL, that's what this was.

Jo swallowed the urge to tell Investigator Cooper Maxwell, the chauvinistic groper, exactly what she thought of him, and held out her hand as cool as a queen.

Which, considering the behavior that had put her in this position, said something heroic about her ability to learn from her mistakes.

"How are you?" she said.

As she expected, he didn't reply when he shook her hand, but looked at the man she'd been introduced to earlier as Lieutenant Norgard. There was no way on God's green earth she was going to bring up that dance or her own humiliating response to him. He'd throw it in her face, use it as a weapon in front of other investigators, and before you knew it, she'd be fighting for her rep up here, too, the way she'd been fighting for nearly a year in L.A.

She should know better than to give in to her body's physical responses. In fact, with a strict regimen of diet and kickboxing and training for a local charity run, she'd thought she had her body pretty much under control. It wasn't her fault she hadn't been in a man's arms—well, except for her trainer, and he didn't count—in so long she'd nearly forgotten how it felt. A woman trying to get ahead in law enforcement didn't have a lot of time for learning dance steps and hanging around at social occasions. The only reason she was at this one was because this investigation had to hit the ground running, and they didn't have time to wait until office hours on Monday.

Not to mention the fact that Jo had had to get out of Dodge before somebody got fired. Like…her.

"I recommend we leave as soon as possible and meet in Santa Rita," Norgard said, taking charge since it was his jurisdiction. "We rented a safe house there, 144 Vista Mar, on the west side. I'll brief you all and Maxwell and MacPherson can get to work tonight."

"Tonight?" Cooper said.

Norgard cocked an eyebrow at him. "You got a hot date, Investigator?"

"No, sir. I have had four beers, though."

"Then you'll collect your stuff from your hotel and ride with me."

"I came down with one of my teammates from narcotics. I'll just let him know."

"My car's parked on the drive. Meet you in ten minutes."

The men scattered and Jo looked at Bella. "You knew he was CLEU, didn't you? How could you do that to me?"

Her sergeant placed a hand on her chest in maidenly protest. "I did not. I had no idea. I just thought you might loosen up a little before we get into Stress Central in this investigation. You have to admit, Jo, he is an attractive guy."

"If you like men who think they're God's gift to women. Which, as you know, I do not. Plus, he groped me, Bella, right out there on the dance floor. Like I haven't had enough humiliation lately."

"This investigation will make up for it," Bella assured her. "You come through on this one and the, er, incident will be expunged from your record. I have it from the unit commander himself. In writing."

"No pressure there." Jo swallowed to moisten her dry throat. "Can't you give me any dirt on what this case is about?"

"We'll get everything at the briefing. Come on."

"One more chocolate-covered strawberry, okay? It'll probably be the last nice thing to happen to me for the next month."

"That's what I like about you, Jo," her sergeant said as they raided the dessert table one last time. "You're such an optimist."

THE SAFE HOUSE on Vista Mar was a World War II-era bungalow covered in white stucco and bearing demure green shutters. It was the kind of unassuming place that an older couple on a limited income might own, or a pair of newlyweds just starting out. It also had a driveway that went all the way to a large separate garage in the back, hidden cameras over each door, and a bank of surveillance and communications equipment in the guest room that would have turned an FBI IT guy sulky with envy.

Maxwell and Norgard were already seated when Jo

and Bella arrived. The Formica-covered kitchen table had been pulled away from the wall and a neat manila folder lay at each setting in lieu of a place mat. Jo seated herself across from Cooper Maxwell, picked hers up and began to leaf through it as Norgard spoke.

"Over the last week, we've seen a rise in sexual assaults in the Santa Rita and local beach resort area. Two have been reported by the local hospital as rape, and three were reported by the victims themselves to the P.D."

"That doesn't seem to fall into CLEU's bailiwick," Cooper commented as he flipped slowly through his folder. "Sounds like the locals should handle it. How do we come in?"

"We come in because the M.O. seems to be connected to several cases scattered all over the state," Bella answered. "Ever hear of the Eros Energy Institute?"

Both Jo and Cooper shook their heads.

"Afrodita Enterprises?"

"Eros and Aphrodite were deities the ancient Greeks associated with sexual love," Cooper said. "Is that some kind of connection?"

"Close." Norgard took up the briefing. "You'll note the incorporation papers of each company in your folder there. Complete with fake names on the boards of directors."

"What do these companies do?" Jo scanned the papers in front of her. "Looks like some kind of educational group."

"Good call," Norgard said. "The companies rent classroom space for their workshops from convention centers and university extensions and the like. The classes run for a couple of weeks, then the company folds up shop and moves on."

"But where's the criminal activity?" Cooper wanted to know. "Sounds like normal operation for that kind of small business."

"Oh, the workshops aren't what worry us," Norgard said. "It's the rise in criminal behavior in each location afterward. Sexual assaults. Rapes. We're trying to head it off before it escalates to murder."

"Wait a minute." Jo closed her folder. "How are you tying these educational classes to sex crimes or homicide? Seems like a long shot to me."

"Not if you know what they're teaching. Are you familiar with alternative health practices that involve the energy meridians of the body?"

"No, but my college roommate was. The flow of chi, she called it."

"This is something different. The meridians these people are interested in involve some kind of blockage to a woman's natural conditioning about men and or strangers. The workshops teach a series of crackpot theories called the Rules of Seduction."

Jo felt her jaw drop. "You're kidding me."

"They're serious, and so are we," Bella said. "These workshops teach men exclusively—no women allowed— how to break down a woman's natural barriers, which does nothing more than set her up to be sexually assaulted. Every town these classes have been taught in has experienced a subsequent rise in their crimes-against-persons rate. Which is why we've been called in. Santa Rita appears to be in the first stages of such a crime wave, and we want you two to get to the bottom of it and stop it."

"What, you mean march into one of these classes and arrest the lot of them? Take down the teacher?" Cooper wanted to know. "Why doesn't the local P.D. just have their business license suspended and disband the workshops?"

"Because they'll just pop up again in a different county two hundred miles away," Norgard said patiently. "We want you two undercover to find out what they're teaching, identify who is taking these so-called lessons to the streets and stop them. And while you're at it, I want you to find out who's behind the dummy companies, scuttle the whole operation and bring him or her up on charges that will stick."

"If these classes are for men only, what do I get to do?" Jo asked. Sit around and type up Cooper Maxwell's notes? Hell would freeze over first."

"You'll be busy, never fear," Norgard said.

"How?"

"These guys are practicing what they've learned on unsuspecting women, Jo," Bella said. "So guess what. You get to be the bait."

Jo leaned forward, interested, and distinctly saw Cooper's gaze drop to the low but still tasteful neckline of her summer dress.

Typical. She could have predicted that. Nothing to do but ignore it.

"So according to what I see here in the file, the perpetrators go to local bars and clubs and hit on women. How do I know if someone is using these Rules of Seduction and it's not just some random loser?"

"There are a couple of statements from recent victims in your folder," Norgard said. "They describe in very basic terms the way these men approached them."

Bella turned a couple of pages. "'He stroked my wrist and asked me if I wanted to go swimming,' the complainant stated." She looked up to meet Jo's eyes. "Not a lot to go on, but it's unusual. You'd pick up on something that much out of the ordinary."

"That weird, you mean," Jo said flatly. "What kind of nutcases are these? And what's the deal with these Rules?"

"That's where Cooper comes in," Norgard said. "These classes aren't advertised, but they do have a Web presence. It comes and goes, but it's there."

"So I should be trolling chat rooms and MySpace to see if I can get a line on a workshop happening here." Cooper made some notes on the cover of his folder. "Then what? Sign up?"

"Yes," Norgard told him. "You'll wear a wire, too, so we have the information on record."

"And get a class roster while you're at it," Jo suggested. "That way we'll have a ready-made list of suspect names if they start doing field trips."

"Good thinking." Norgard smiled at her and Jo straightened her back as the warmth of his approval spread through her.

She'd learned long ago that using her feminine gifts to get attention only relegated her to the passenger's seat in life—always going along for the ride and never getting to drive. As a military brat, she'd watched her dad with the men and women in his command, and invariably it was the women who came off as one of the boys, who used their brains and physical strength to succeed, who connected best with him. So she'd learned to do that, too, much to her mom's dismay. No curling ringlets and frilly dresses for Joanna MacPherson, uh-uh. She wore jeans and sneakers and kept her hair short, and learned to give as good as she got. Her reward was a rare smile from Dad, and a renewed determination to make up for being just a girl—never quite enough, never quite what he expected.

It hadn't served her so badly, either. She'd gravitated naturally to a field where she could continue her unspoken competition with men, and she'd done well at it. She'd graduated from the academy first in her class, and had been seconded to CLEU four years after joining LAPD. She liked pitting her wits not only against her coworkers and supervising officers, but against the lowlifes on the streets during undercover operations.

"Class roster." Cooper spoke absently as he wrote it down. "Anything else?"

"Yes." Bella caught Jo's eye. "Be careful, Jo. Six months ago in Sacramento there was a serial rapist out there with ties to this Rules of Seduction thing. We never caught him, and none of his victims were able to give us a concrete description. If you're going to be on the street, I want Cooper and at least one other operator in sight at all times as your cover team."

"Both of them?" Cooper Maxwell could just toddle off to his little seduction classes and leave her alone to do her job. "Is that necessary? I can take care of myself."

"We're talking rape, Jo. I don't want you anywhere near that kind of scenario."

"I'd like to see him try," Jo scoffed. "I'll put him in the hospital, the way I put—"

"Investigator!"

As Bella cut her off, Jo shut her mouth, but it was too late. Both Norgard and Cooper Maxwell were pretending to study the contents of their folders, but ten to one they'd both hustle to the nearest computer to find out all the juicy details. A half hint like that was too good to leave lying.

Fine. Let them. All they'd find out was that she'd nearly been suspended for putting Anthony "Bling" Bingham in the hospital with a couple of fractures and a nice concussion. He'd deserved it and she wasn't sorry. The fifteen-year-old sister of her college roommate— she who knew about energy meridians and such—had run away to L.A. to seek her fortune and had met up with Bling instead. He had still been softening her up to a life of prostitution when Jo had caught up with her.

And then things had gotten personal between Jo and Bling.

The only thing she was sorry about was getting shipped up here to play The Girl for these guys. Well, she'd show them. She was capable of much more than playing the silent girlfriend, the window dressing that made the targets feel nice and comfortable before the investigators took them down.

"On a different subject," Bella said, ever the diplomat, "let's talk about logistics. Where is my investigator staying? Our per diem budget is limited, but since Santa Rita is a beach town, we should be able to get a motel room at a pretty reasonable rate."

"Motel room?" Norgard gestured around the kitchen. "What's wrong with this? It's good enough for Coop, here. It should be good enough for your operator."

Bella narrowed her gaze at him. "I trust you haven't forgotten the CLEU policy against operators of different sexes sharing quarters, Lieutenant."

"Of course not. Maybe in L.A. the state's pockets are fatter, but here in Northern California our field budget doesn't allow for unlimited hotel stays, especially now at peak season. That's why we have the lease on this place. My surveillance crew consists of a man and a woman, Sergeant. They'll be arriving this afternoon, in time to wire Investigator MacPherson here for her shift tonight. We'll put MacPherson with Leah Martinez and Coop will bunk with Will Stutz. Simple."

Bella looked over at her. "Is that arrangement satisfactory, Jo?"

I'm not staying in the same house with Cooper Maxwell. I'd rather sleep on the beach.

As if he'd heard the screaming in her head, Cooper tilted his chair back, crossed his arms over his broad chest and grinned at her.

Chicken, that grin said. *I'm too much man for you, aren't I? Go on. Run away and get your own room. I dare you.*

Jo MacPherson had never backed down from a challenge in her life.

"Perfectly satisfactory," she said, acutely conscious that Cooper was watching her lips move as she enunciated every syllable.

And enjoying it way too much.

4

144 Vista Mar
Santa Rita, California
18:47 hours

COOPER'S FINGERS DANCED over the keys of the computer in the comm room, tracking the adherents of the Rules through cyberspace like the electronic equivalent of a bloodhound on a scent. Half his brain concentrated on the information on the wide display screen while the other half catalogued every movement, every breath, of the woman standing behind his chair.

After Lieutenant Norgard and Sergeant Waring had left, one heading for San Francisco and the other for Los Angeles, she'd gone into one of the bedrooms and changed into practical jeans and one of the white T-shirts they'd all been issued at the academy. The California Law Enforcement Unit shield on the chest took on a number of highly interesting properties when she wore it.

She leaned over the back of his chair and he lost his concentration. "So, how exactly are you approaching this?"

She didn't wear perfume. Still, the scent of lime and clean cotton seemed to emanate from her. He took a deep breath. Shampoo, maybe? Moisturizer of some kind? She was now his partner and therefore all lusty thoughts had to be sent to a locked cell in his brain. So, he'd limit himself to simple, undetectable pleasures, like breathing.

"I applied some profiling elements to an imaginary guy. I asked myself, what kind of person would need to take a class to learn how to seduce a woman?"

"A total loser?" she suggested.

"We need to be more specific," he said dryly. "What kind of guy is socially inept, maybe emotionally closed off, and tends to operate with his head more than his heart? What kind of guy would see taking a class as a solution instead of going to a baseball game or joining the Sierra Club to meet people?"

"Someone with more intelligence than is good for him? Like an engineer or something?"

"Exactly." Cooper indicated the screen. "So here's where I started. UC Santa Rita is an engineering school. This is an alumni chat room."

He logged in and watched an ongoing conversation scroll by.

"LimeBoy?" Jo said incredulously. "What kind of a screen name is that?"

He shrugged "I just made it up. I'm not going to use my real screen name for something like this."

"And what would that be?"

He glanced over his shoulder at her. "Can't tell you. We could meet up on a chat list somewhere and then you'd know who I was."

"God forbid we'd be on the same lists." She straightened and crossed her arms. "That would mean being interested in the same things. And then hell would freeze over."

More chat room conversation rolled past. "Are you on the CLEU investigators' loop?"

"Of course."

"Do I hear the sound of lava freezing?"

"Very funny."

"Don't be so quick to—" He stopped. "Hey."

Joanna grabbed the chair in front of the video monitor and scooted it closer to him. "What?"

"They're talking about Atlantis. That's the local meat market."

Amino127:   Nice place, good music. Food could be better though.

DNDwizard: Who cares about food? Any action?

Orphan: Depends.

DNDwizard: On what?

Orphan: The night you go. And other things.

DNDwizard: What other things?

Amino127:   Whether you've been to class or not, heh.

DNDwizard: Don't get it.

Orphan: Tease.

DNDwizard: Still don't get it.

LimeBoy: Class?

Amino127:   To learn the rules.

DNDwizard: I'm outta here. Pricks.

:: DNDwizard has left the chat room 18:57 ::

Amino127:   Quitter.

LimeBoy: I'm no quitter. Interested in learning.

Orphan: Check out eropsych.com

Amino127:   GTG

:: Amino127 has left the chat room 18:58 ::

LimeBoy: Do you know the rules?

Orphan: Yep.

LimeBoy: Do they work?

Orphan: Yep.

LimeBoy: How?

Orphan: Check the site. You'll see. More ass
than a toilet seat. Your choice and no dogs either.

LimeBoy:	Sounds good. Tx.

Orphan:	NP

:: LimeBoy has left the chat room 19:00 ::

Jo tilted her chair back and regarded the screen sourly. "It's heartening to know the respect that the American woman commands among the men of our nation."

"I'd say Orphan definitely has problems relating on an emotional level," Cooper allowed.

"He's a pig."

"Maybe he's really an orphan. That would account for some of it."

"Or maybe he's just a pig, like the rest."

Cooper raised his eyebrows. "Speaking of trouble relating on an emotional level…"

A scarlet flush swamped the dusting of freckles over her nose and cheekbones. "Let's get one thing straight right off the bat, Maxwell," she said in a low tone, though they were the only ones in the house. "I've got your number. You lost my respect the minute you groped me at that wedding. You stay out of my personal life and I'll stay out of yours."

He hadn't entertained a single thought about invading her personal life. Who would want to hook up with a cranky cat like this, anyway? All he'd wanted to do was enjoy a brief night with her. Now you couldn't pay him to think that way.

"Not a problem," he said evenly. "And I did apologize."

"Only after you found out I was a cop. If I'd been your run-of-the-mill wedding guest, you'd have written me off and never bothered."

He typed www.eropsych.com into the navigation bar. "I'd be careful about making too many assumptions without proof, Investigator. Not a good way to make a case."

She snorted. "I had all the proof I needed. And probably a bruise, too."

He considered keeping quiet and maintaining a professional demeanor for about a millisecond. "Not likely. But it was a fine butt."

Her heels smacked the floor as she pushed her chair back. "Maxwell!"

"Just an observation."

"I don't want any more observations like that out of you. It's inappropriate."

"I know. But true."

"Save it." She took a couple of deep breaths. "Can we work now? Is that the Web site?"

The corners of his mouth twitched. She might be out of bounds, but she was still magnificent when she was angry. Item one at the top of his personal to-do list was to find out what exactly had happened to put her on— as she so elegantly put it—this punishment detail. He'd bet his next paycheck it had something to do with her lack of impulse control.

The Web site had been hastily constructed from a basic business template, and contained only one page. If they'd just happened across it, he would never have recognized it for what it was. All it contained was a list of dates, times and places, with a contact e-mail address.

Not even a phone number that they could cross-reference to a storefront or physical address.

"There," Joanna said. "Santa Rita, June twenty-first. Nine to five Monday and Tuesday at the West Side Community Center."

"That's the day after tomorrow. Looks like we got lucky."

"There's another class." She pointed at the one listed for San Jose. "But it's a week away, and who knows how many women could be in the hospital by then."

"What I'd like to know is what connects this energy flow stuff they're teaching with the rise in violence," Cooper mused. "I'm no doctor, but if these guys are messing with the women's energy, why are the women winding up in Emergency? It's not like your flow of chi is breakable."

"I guess you'll find out in the class." With a shove, she rolled the chair back to its place in front of the video bank and got up. "Meantime, I'm going out."

"Where?"

"I need to pick up a few things at the drugstore. And I want to drive around a little and get my bearings. I assume we have a department vehicle to use?"

He jerked a thumb in the direction of the back of the house. "It's in the garage. Be back by eight. We need to huddle with Will Stutz when he comes on shift, and plan out a strategy for tonight."

Her nod was businesslike in the extreme. She collected her handbag and the car keys, and left the house without another look in his direction.

The door had barely closed behind her when he turned back to the screen and logged into the CLEU interface. Some months ago his former narcotics team had hacked the human resources database, just to see if they could. They hadn't meant anything malicious by it—it was more of a mental exercise, to keep their skills sharp. And sure enough, it had opened up like a willing woman under the blandishment of Danny Kowalski's fingers.

Joanna backed out of the driveway, blissfully unaware that her personnel file was telling tales on his desktop. The most recent entry was dated only the past Wednesday.

Employee assured Dr. Hayward that she would sign up for an anger management class at the earliest opportunity.

She'd been sent up here a couple of days later, so that hadn't happened. Coop made a mental note to brush up on his self-defense moves, just in case. He clicked the mouse, scrolling further into the record.

I feel this department is not meeting the needs of Investigator MacPherson.
Request a secondary evaluation and ongoing counseling.

Investigator did not show up for our scheduled session.

Investigator seemed impatient at the need for these appointments and repeatedly asked why they were necessary.

Investigator has issues with male authority,
possibly stemming from her relationship with her
father, who is a navy admiral.

Investigator advises that her physical injuries have
healed while on administrative leave, and requests
permission to return to active duty.

What? Cooper clicked faster and came to what
looked like a hospital report on one Anthony James
Bingham. Concussion, fractured tibia, broken wrist.

Joanna had been put on forced leave for beating on
the guy? With two more clicks, Coop flipped into
NCIS and brought up Bingham's record. Ah. He had
been a pimp, with numerous petty drug and theft
charges. Something big must have happened to set
her off.

He backed out of the interface, erased its history and
closed all but an innocuous Web browser. Punishment
detail, huh? If he hadn't been so curious, he'd be
offended. Why would they put an investigator with a
history of violence on a case that involved assaults
against women? Did the powers that be think she'd be
more motivated to succeed? In his opinion, it would just
give her more to be angry about.

He'd been a little flippant about working with her
before. It had been a challenge to him, despite their
rocky beginning and her obviously low opinion of him
as a man. Now he wasn't sure how he felt.

Under any circumstance, he needed to be able to
depend on his partner, to know that she would do the
right thing no matter what the provocation. How could

he trust her with his life when she couldn't even be trusted with a man's tibias?

"I JUST DON'T TRUST the guy."

Joanna made a right turn into the drugstore's parking lot and spoke into her cell phone. Carleen Perez had been her confidante in college, her best friend through her days at the academy and, now that they were both established in their careers, the person she turned to for a listening ear.

"Give him a chance, Jo," Carleen said. "Not every guy is a Michael Dunn or an Anthony Bingham."

"I still can't believe Michael actually moved to Florida instead of just calling me and breaking it off. What did he think I was going to do, hunt him down and kill him?"

"Uh, maybe." Carleen paused. "We agree he's cowardly scum. But it's been, what, eighteen months? One of these days you're going to find the cure to that guy."

"I don't have time to look."

"I don't think you want to look. All this trouble you get into is just an excuse."

There were times when Carleen was too honest for Joanna's own good. "All right, smart mouth, spill. An excuse for what?"

"For not getting involved. For not making yourself vulnerable."

"Only a stupid woman makes herself vulnerable to a man on purpose." She pushed open the drugstore's glass and metal door and headed for the aisle that held headache tablets.

"Says you. But when you trust someone and learn to love him, it comes naturally."

"Not for me."

"It will, Joanna. There's hope for you. I mean, you trust me and tell me stuff that makes you vulnerable, right?"

"You're a nurse. And we've been best buds for ten years. Of course I trust you. That's different." Headache tablets, bottled water, soap. What else?

"Like I said, it's a start. Give this guy Cooper a chance."

"I have no intention of getting into a relationship with him."

"Of course not." Carleen's tone was soothing. "He's your partner. It's not an issue. I'm just saying, maybe you can use him for practice in trusting on a purely official level. That's what partners are all about, right?"

"Supposedly. Although Wade didn't waste any time in hanging me out to dry over Bling."

"Uh-huh. And who had spent six months doing nothing but competing and putting him down and generally driving the guy into a rage?"

"I didn't drive Wade into a rage. And a little healthy competition is good for him."

"A little might be, but you took that poor guy to the wall. Geez, Joanna, when are you going to learn moderation?"

"Moderation doesn't get the job done. I give it all I've got and sometimes people don't move out of the way fast enough."

"You sound like that guy in *Lethal Weapon*. The Mel Gibson character."

One of Jo's favorite movies. "Except I don't have a death wish."

"Maybe not, but you've got something else going on. I'm serious, Jo. You need to learn to manage this somehow."

"I just need about twelve hours of sex, is all."

At the end of the aisle, a guy choosing cold medicine straightened and looked at her. She whipped around the corner and grabbed a bottle of shampoo.

"Oh, is that the problem? Good grief, Jo, why don't you just keep a boy toy in your apartment instead of littering the landscape with damaged men?"

"If anyone is going to be living in my apartment, it'll be because I respect him and want him to be there. Not because he's there for sex." She stepped behind a display of plastic tubs. "Besides, if all I wanted was sex, I'd be in clover. Maxwell already made it plain that's what he wanted."

"Well, then?"

"Well, nothing. You just said it's a nonissue while he and I are working together."

"You don't sound convinced."

Joanna snorted. "Believe me, I am. He's the last guy I'd climb into bed with."

"Even though you said dancing with him was pretty hot."

"That was before he groped me."

"Even so, you admit there was chemistry there."

"Yes, maybe," Joanna said reluctantly. "For about a minute and a half."

"Congratulations, Joanna MacPherson. You've just discovered you're still a woman."

"Ha ha. Very funny."

"Don't knock it. You're in a male-dominated profession, surrounded by men who are off-limits. You're in constant competition with them to the point where you forget you're even female. I think that remembering that fact for even a minute and a half is significant."

Joanna said something very pithy that made the little old lady examining the hair products in the next aisle gawk at her and skitter away.

But Carleen wasn't finished yet. "There must be something unusual about this guy Cooper, partner or not. He makes you *feel*. Give the man a gold star."

"I'm so glad to see you're on my side once again, Carleen."

"Always. You know that. You got my baby sister home safely. I'm yours for life."

"And I'm glad to hear it." With Carleen, she could be completely honest. "If I didn't have you to vent to, I'd probably—"

"Hurt something?"

"Yeah." She paused. "Unfortunately, most of the time it's myself."

5

WHEN JOANNA GOT back to the safe house, she was glad she'd stopped for a homemade chile relleno burrito at a hole in the wall across from Atlantis. A pizza box from a chain sat on the kitchen table, greasy pepperoni congealing as it cooled.

Bleah. Give her authentic ethnic food any day—something tasty and full of character.

"You must be Joanna MacPherson." A kid in his twenties with a bleached-blond surfer haircut came out of the comm room. He held out a hand. "Will Stutz."

"Nice to meet you, Will. I understand you're on our team."

"My first undercover." He glowed like a girl who has just been asked to the prom. That smile was a knockout—if she were interested in robbing the cradle. "I've been working the comm systems and doing support for a couple of years, but this is the first time my request for an undercover has been approved." He waved at the pizza box. "Did you eat?"

She nodded. "I grabbed a burrito on the way over. Is Maxwell here?"

"In here."

Joanna followed the sound of Cooper's voice into the comm room, where, from the look of the form on the screen in front of him, he had been updating the case file online.

"Are we ready to brief?"

He closed the report as Will joined them. "When you are."

She tossed the plastic bag containing her purchases in her room, and stopped in midswing. The young woman standing at the end of the second bed yanked a T-shirt over her head and tucked it into her jeans.

"You must be Leah Martinez."

"And you're Joanna MacPherson." They shook hands. "I'll be doing dispatch for you tonight while the boys cover you."

"They're ready to brief."

"Let's get some sodas."

After a stop at the fridge, all four investigators settled around the kitchen table. Cooper moved the pizza box to the counter, much to Joanna's relief. He couldn't know about her aversion to cardboard pepperoni, but it was considerate of him anyway.

"I've been designated the lead for this case, and Joanna is my secondary," Cooper began. "If I'm off the air, you guys will take orders from her."

Will and Leah nodded.

"We're going to do a preliminary scout of a couple of the clubs downtown to see if anyone will approach

Joanna using these Rules. I assume you've both read the case reports?"

"This is some kind of mental interference using energy meridians?" Leah said. "It's a stretch for me. I'm better with stolen property or narcotics."

"We'll know more after Tuesday," Joanna put in, and glanced at Cooper. "Were you able to get into one of those classes?"

He nodded. "I signed up, no problem. Norgard is going to choke when he sees the fee. Fifteen hundred bucks for a two-day class."

"It's a scam, then," Leah said flatly. "On top of everything else."

"Probably," Cooper agreed. "But it's our scam. So tonight, we'll concentrate on people who approach Joanna. ID, vehicles, whatever we can get. Leah, I need you to call the local hospitals to see if any women are admitted tonight or tomorrow with injuries consistent with assault. You and Joanna can interview them while I'm in class." He looked at Will, who sat across from Joanna. "Do you have a list of the clubs and bars here? We should start with three or four."

Will pushed a sheet of paper toward him. On it was a close-up satellite photo of downtown Santa Rita. "The blue circles are bars, the red ones clubs."

"And the yellow ones?" Leah peered at the 3-D map.

Will grinned. "Restaurants and places with public bathrooms. Just in case this turns into a surveillance."

Joanna smiled. The kid's enthusiasm was contagious and a little touching. She'd been like that, once. Bright and filled with ideas, impatient to get out there and start cleaning up the streets. What had happened to that girl, anyway? What had made her this angry, sarcastic bitch who chewed men up and put them into hospital?

She frowned and pushed the thought aside. "Anything else we need to know?"

"We'll start at the Pink Salamander bar at nine, and if nothing happens, we'll move on to Club Koko, here." He pointed to a red circle about half a block from a blue one. "On the next block is the Harp and Saddle, and finally, we'll hit Atlantis around midnight."

Will spoke up. "These are all locations where women have reported being picked up in the past. Unfortunately, none of them could give us a specific description of the guy or guys. They remembered general height and coloring, but when it came to picking out a mug shot or giving a description to a police artist, they went blank."

"Are these women being brainwashed?" Joanna asked. "Or hypnotized?"

"I guess you'll find out," Will said.

Not for the first time, Joanna was grateful for the policy that dictated the presence of a cover team for every operator. Maybe she'd been just the tiniest bit hard on Cooper Maxwell. She found herself hoping that he wouldn't hold it against her when she was being hypnotized in a bar by a crazy guy.

"So, what are you going to wear?" Leah wanted to know as the two of them went back to their room.

Joanna closed the door behind them. "I was thinking something fairly casual. This is a beach town, not Hollywood, so maybe my cropped cargo pants and a tank top."

"Can you wear a shirt or something over it?" Leah

held up a flat transmitter and a microphone. "I have to wire you."

"Better than that." Joanna pulled an olive green silk top out of her suitcase. "This isn't skin tight, it's got a low neckline but it's kind of loose, too."

"Perfect. Let's get you taped up."

Leah was good. In less than ten minutes, Joanna was wired, taped and dressed, with a discreet wireless transmitter bud fitted in her ear. Since she'd started with CLEU, she kept her hair short enough to be low maintenance and long enough to cover such things. A chunky necklace drew attention to her cleavage, and her sandals had a practical heel in case she needed to stomp someone's instep.

No, no, no. She really had to stop thinking that way.

Correction. In case she needed to make a quick exit.

With a final application of makeup, she was done. When she walked into the comm room, Will sat up and stared, then collected himself, nodded and turned back to the computer screen. Cooper, however, didn't have his discretion.

"Very nice," he said on a long note of appreciation. "That ought to bring them in like trout to a wet fly."

Joanna refused to be baited, much less even a little bit pleased that he liked what he saw. Who knew if he was being sincere?

"That's the point, right?" she said lightly. "Everyone ready?"

Cooper inserted his own transmitter in his ear. "As we'll ever be. Time to go fishing."

If she'd been at home in L.A., the Pink Salamander would have been just her kind of place. Lots of windows and shining brass and wood that hadn't had the initials of countless idiots carved into it over time. Cocktails in jewel tones and decent dance music spun by the DJ on the ministage in the corner.

But she wasn't at home, and she couldn't meet Carleen here. She had to act seductive and interested with anyone who happened to pull up a stool next to her at the bar.

So not her usual modus operandi.

Not that she didn't know how to be seductive, or that she didn't find men interesting. But playing such a part in the context of work was so out of her usual range she just hoped she could pull it off convincingly. Take down a drug dealer? Sure. Book a burglar? No problem. But smile into the face of every hopeful looking to get laid?

Not so much.

She ordered a light beer while Will and Cooper settled at a table just behind her, close enough to hear conversations but far enough away that they wouldn't arouse suspicion by listening. Not fifteen minutes after the waitress had taken their order, she came back.

"Excuse me, gentlemen, but those ladies over by the window—" two women in their late thirties waved cheerily "—would like to buy each of you a drink."

Joanna choked on her beer and slapped a napkin against her mouth. *Do not laugh. Not yet. Oh, they are never going to hear the end of this.*

It took Cooper a moment to recover, too. "Uh, thank the ladies very much, but we can't accept."

She walked away and Joanna mustered every ounce of self-control she had not to turn around and rib them mercilessly. By the time she managed to quell the urge, the waitress had come back. "I'm afraid they're insist-

ing." She put two beers on the table—two beers that two
working cops absolutely could not consume and be able
to drive a state-owned vehicle afterward.

Cooper and Will looked at each other, and waved
weakly in thanks to the two women by the window. As the
waitress walked past the bar, Joanna motioned her over.

"You might just drop a hint to the ladies that these
two are, uh, unavailable," she said in a voice pitched just
low enough for Cooper, who had his back to her, to hear.
"To women in general, I mean."

"Yeah?" The waitress looked a little sorry to hear it.

"I overheard their conversation a minute ago. I would
definitely say so—it sounds to me like they're on a date."

"Okay," the waitress said. "I'll pass it along. Waste
of two beers, I guess."

Joanna didn't dare turn around, but her shoulders
shook as she laughed silently into her own mug.

*Cooper Maxwell, consider the score officially evened
up.*

And the grope officially forgotten.

It was satisfying to know that there was nothing
Cooper or Will could do about it as long as they were
on the job. Tonight, back at the safe house? Well, she'd
worry about it then.

For now, it was time to make herself visible. She
picked up her handbag and sashayed toward the ladies'
room at the back of the bar, making her hips sway a
touch more than usual.

And it worked. At least four male gazes tracked her
progress. Maybe she'd see some action when she came
back.

After she'd used the facilities and was washing her

hands, the door opened and two young women in their twenties came in, giggling. One wore jeans and a sparkly top, and the other a burgundy silk dress with a chiffon overlay that floated around her. The girls leaned over the sink and began to fix their makeup.

"This is so much fun, Danielle," the girl in jeans said. "I totally love being legal—though the bartender carded me. I think he did it on purpose."

"He just wanted to make sure you weren't jail bait before he hit on you," Danielle said.

"Which totally won't happen. We're here for you. This deserves an all-night celebration before you have to buckle down and be an adult on Monday."

"What are you celebrating?" Joanna asked with a smile as she looked at them in the mirror.

Danielle's eyes sparkled enough to rival the gold, snake-shaped pendant she wore. "I landed a job at Starfish Software and I only just graduated from UCSR, like, last week. They're totally the coolest place to work on the central coast. I'm going to be a junior software developer for visual effects."

"Congratulations!" Joanna said. "Does that mean I'll be seeing your work at the movies?"

The girl in jeans grinned. "We hope." She outlined the shape of a movie screen in the air. "Watch the credits roll, and there she is—Visual Effects Supervisor: Danielle. Woo-hoo!"

Joanna laughed and left the restroom as the girls continued to chatter. When she got back to her seat, she prepared herself to be approached by one of the men who had been eyeing her, but by the time she'd finished her drink, nothing had happened.

At nine forty-five, Cooper caught Joanna's eye and glanced at his watch. Effectively declaring the Pink Salamander a bust, the men left the bar and, five minutes later, Joanna did the same. She breathed in the scents of a soft summer evening as she strolled toward Club Koko—the scent of the ocean a few blocks away mixed with the tang of grilled beef from a restaurant and warm sugar from an ice cream parlor.

"Vista Base to Joanna," Leah's voice said in her ear. "Cooper and Will are set up inside location two. They say there's one seat left at the bar and the prospects look good."

"Acknowledged," Joanna murmured.

"They also request no more fictionalizing. What does that mean?"

Joanna snickered. "Tell you later."

"Ten-four. Good luck. Vista Base out."

She strolled into the bar as if she owned the place. Again, her hips swung a degree more than usual, and she straightened her spine, giving her breasts some attention-getting definition. She slid into the last seat at the bar and noted with satisfaction that several male heads had turned her way.

This was more like it. *Come on, boys, let's get down to business.*

Cooper and Will sat a little farther away than before, but everything she said would be captured on the wire and rebroadcast to them in real time. It meant she couldn't make any more jokes at their expense, but the time for jokes was past. It looked like she'd be getting some serious Rules-type action any minute now.

Sure enough, a guy got up from a table across the

room and touched her on the shoulder, right where the tendon stretched from neck to bone.

"If you're not expecting anyone, you're welcome to join me at my table," he said.

In a caress as light as thought, his finger traveled up the tendon to the back of her neck. Why not? Joanna thought.

"That would be nice," she said.

She followed him, giving the waitress her order in a low tone on the way: a nonalcoholic beer, in a frosted mug. At the table, he held her chair for her, and as she seated herself, again she felt that light touch on the nape of her neck.

Goose bumps prickled over her shoulders.

"I've never been to this place before," she said. "Is it always this busy?"

"It's a pretty popular spot. A lot of people meet friends here—or make new ones. I find it doesn't take long to connect with someone who enjoys the same things I do." He slid a warm hand under hers, his fingers touching her wrist. "That's a very distinctive necklace you have on. Uninhibited. Sexy."

He had great eyes, with an appealing twinkle. Surely a guy like this wouldn't turn out to be violent. "I like it."

"I do, too. It tells me the kind of woman you are, and I like that. Very much."

Too bad she was on the job. Carleen would probably say this was exactly the kind of guy she should hook up with.

"Let's go somewhere quieter," he suggested. "Where we can get to know each other better."

"Okay."

"Joanna!" Leah said urgently in her ear. "Joanna, you're not supposed to go anywhere. Get his name!"

What was the problem with going somewhere else? The team could follow her. Besides, maybe once the job was done they could reconnect. She should get his card.

"Investigator, disengage! Joanna, is your unit operating?"

She barely restrained herself from rolling her eyes. *Come on, Leah, go with the flow. Don't be such a hardnose about the rules.*

At the door, Will and Cooper jostled her date and he let go of her hand. "Sorry I was late, darling," Cooper said. She stared at him in amazement. What was he doing, butting in just when she was getting somewhere? He kissed her on the cheek, tucked her hand into the crook of his arm and hustled her out of the bar while Will talked for a few seconds with the man with the nice smile.

Damn. She should have got his name and his phone number while she had the chance.

"Are you all right?"

She blinked at the real concern in his tone. What was the matter with him? Did he think she'd been in some kind of danger? Why, the guy was a sweetheart, she'd bet money on it.

"Joanna? Did he use the Rules on you?"

"Of course not," she said instantly. "He was just being nice."

"Yeah, I bet." He held open the door of a dark green Ford Taurus and bundled her into it while Will ambled down the street.

"Geez, Joanna, don't scare us like that," Cooper said. "What happened to our strategy?"

The complacent sense of well-being, of acceptance, seemed to part and roll away. "What strategy? I was getting somewhere until you guys decided to step in and mess it up."

Frowning, Cooper held up a finger. "Track this."

She slapped his hand away. "Give me a break. What's wrong with you?"

"I have Joanna safely in the police vehicle," Cooper told Leah. "All clear." To Joanna, he said, "Do you mind explaining the last five minutes to me?"

"I don't know what needs explaining. He was a nice guy. We talked for a minute and he suggested going somewhere quieter." She paused, and a chill wavered over her skin. "And I totally had no problem going off with a stranger and leaving my cover team. Did he use the Rules on me?"

He nodded. "Looks like it." He touched the transmitter in his ear. "Will, do you still have the eye?"

Will's voice, hushed into the quiet register they used on surveillance, sounded in Joanna's ear. "I'm in a parking lot off Third Street, right behind the club. He got into a black Camry, California plate 7DWH447."

"Got it," Leah's voice said. "Registered to a Thomas Semple at a San Jose address." She paused a second, then reported, "No warrants, no convictions. Not even a traffic ticket. Driver's license photo is recent, so I'll print it in case we get any assault victims who might recognize him."

"Good work, guys," Cooper told them. "Come on back to the car, Will. I think Joanna's going to call it a night."

"Why?" Frowning, Joanna faced him across the center console. "There's nothing the matter with me."

"I don't like putting you out there when we don't know anything about the effects these Rules have. Think about it, Joanna. He got a trained investigator to lower her defenses in less than a minute, when she was ready for him and expecting something to happen. There's more to this than meets the eye, and I'm not willing to put you at risk again."

"What risk? You and Will were right there. If I'm willing to try another club, that should be good enough for you."

Will opened the car door and slid into the backseat. "I agree with Cooper."

"You would." Joanna didn't bother to look at him. Cooper was the senior investigator. He was the one she had to convince.

"What's that supposed to mean?" Will sounded injured. "That guy put the mojo on you in thirty seconds. There might be long-term effects, for all we know."

Joanna glared at him through the space between the seats. "Like what? I get the sudden urge to jump the next guy I see?"

"We should be so lucky," Cooper said to no one in particular.

"I might remind you this is a monitored channel and these tapes are being transcribed for the case file," Leah's voice said dryly in three sets of transmitters. "Keep it clean."

Cooper took a deep breath. "As senior investigator, I'm calling it off for tonight. We need to analyze what happened, not make it happen again."

And because he was a man and behind the wheel and

thought he was in control, Joanna had to go along with it. She sat in silence all the way back to the safe house. What was wrong with him? They were wasting time. If someone got hurt and wound up in the hospital tonight, it would be Cooper's fault.

When they arrived, Leah already had the digital file clipped, loaded and ready for the debriefing. Her whole body a silent but visible protest, Joanna joined the others and listened to herself and Tom Semple talking.

That couldn't be her. She sounded like a robot. A Stepford cop. And why couldn't she remember any details? He'd had a nice smile, she remembered thinking that, but her usual ability to estimate height and weight, and to remember eye color, hair color and visible identifiers like scars and moles had vanished like a wiped diskette.

The stiffness of affront drained out of her body, and by the time Cooper's and Will's voices came on, even her knees had gone limp with confusion. She fumbled for a kitchen chair and sank onto it.

Cooper glanced at her. "You okay?"

"This is scary," she admitted. "I can't believe I actually fell for his act so easily. And it really bugs me that I can't remember what he looks like." She glanced at the photo Leah had downloaded. "Without this, I'd be no help at all if I had to give a description."

"That's consistent with the statements of some of the assault victims," Leah said. "They had a general impression, but no details."

"I always get the details," Joanna replied. "That's the scary part. Whatever these Rules are, they make it impossible to do my job."

"Which makes it even more important for me to be in that class on Monday." Cooper touched her hand, and Joanna jerked it away. "We need to know if messing with these energy meridians produces any long-term effects. You're feeling okay now?"

"Perfectly normal, except for the memory loss. And the sense I've let you all down."

Will shook his head. "You haven't. This is all good information. Next time we'll know better. Maybe while Cooper is learning how to put a whammy on a woman, he can find out how to stop one, too."

"I hope so," Joanna said. "Because meanwhile, if we can't depend on me, it'll slow down the investigation."

Leah straightened. "I could do it."

"No." Cooper's tone meant no one got to argue. "Joanna is more experienced than you."

"Yeah, but how do I get experience if I don't work?"

"You pick an operation that's more straightforward than this one," Will told her. "One where the suspects aren't clouding your mind with their superpowers."

"They aren't superpowers," Joanna said. "These are ordinary guys using some physiological technique that we can learn and analyze. No more than that. Meantime, since we can't go back to work, what's our next step?"

"Tomorrow's Sunday," Cooper said. "I vote we take a day off and then get back at it on Monday."

"I vote we go pick up Semple and grill him about what he did to me," Joanna said.

"On what grounds?" Leah wanted to know. "He didn't commit a crime."

"I know that." Joanna's shoulders slumped. "I just

want to know how he did it—and what he planned to do afterward."

"And whether he went somewhere else to try again," Cooper said.

Across the table, Joanna's gaze locked with his. Because at last she understood what it felt like to have her control taken away so completely, without her permission. Whatever these Rules were, the women out there were very much at risk.

And the only thing standing between those women and a rising crime wave was this little team right here in the kitchen. It meant she had to be patient. It meant they needed to get more information.

It meant several more days in the same house with Cooper Maxwell.

6

144 Vista Mar
Santa Rita, California
02:30 hours

JOANNA SIGHED AND put her watch, with its digital alarm and glow-in-the-dark face, back on the nightstand. Maybe it was a good thing Cooper had given them the day off tomorrow…er, today. If she was lucky, she'd fall asleep by five and get three hours before someone got up to put the coffee on.

She knew the reason she couldn't sleep, of course. It was these damned Rules and the effect they'd had on her, shattering her self-confidence.

Unacceptable.

She threw the covers back, careful not to disturb Leah, who was snoring gently in the other bed. After pulling on a sweatshirt over her sleep cami and cotton drawstring pajama bottoms, she slipped out of the room and down the hall to the kitchen. The back door opened silently, and only the camera mounted above it recorded her presence as she walked out into the yard.

Since real people didn't actually live here, the backyard was very low maintenance, with only a postage-stamp-size lawn and some dry-climate plants to one side of it. Most of it was a brickwork patio that extended to a large loquat tree, now fragrant with tight clusters of sweet-smelling, waxy flowers.

The bricks felt cool under her bare feet as she leaned on the trunk of the tree, listening to the boom and whisper of the breakers a couple of streets over.

And the click of the back door closing.

Joanna jerked around. Cooper Maxwell, in a pair of jeans and nothing else, sat on the back step and ran a tired hand through his hair. Then he balanced his arms on his knees and tilted his head back to look at the starry sky.

He hadn't seen her in the gently moving shadows under the tree, and if she didn't move, he wouldn't, either. She didn't want to share her sleeplessness with him—or her possession of the quiet patio. She didn't want to admit to anyone how much her failure this evening had shaken her, and she particularly didn't want this man seeing that kind of weakness. Any minute now he'd get bored and go back in.

Any minute now. Meantime, he'd never know if she checked him out a little. Yes, he was as much of a control freak as she was, and yes, she was his partner under protest, but that didn't mean she couldn't take a moment to appreciate that landscape of bare skin when it was sitting on the step in front of her, right?

The guy had nothing to be ashamed of, that was for sure. His arms and chest were layered with the kind of muscle that might have come from regular workouts with weights, or from fabulous genes, or just from a job that required a man to be at the top of his form. A hard six-pack of abdominals tapered into the waistband of his jeans, which hugged him in all the right places and hinted at power through the hips and thighs. Even his feet looked good as they rested on the concrete step—long and tanned and bare.

What was it they said about a man's big toes? Or was it his thumbs? Hmm. She'd have to ask Carleen. Not that it mattered when you were talking about your partner, but—

"You going to stand there all night?"

His voice was quiet, part of the whisper of the night wind and the distant bass of the breakers, but still it sent a jolt of surprise and guilt through her, as though she'd been caught peeking—or trespassing.

"I might as well." Pretending she'd meant to all along, she crossed the patio and sat on the retaining wall next to the unused barbecue pit. She could stretch out a leg and touch him with a toe—close enough to talk to but not too close. She took a deep breath to calm her pounding heart, and exhaled. "What are you doing up?"

He shrugged, bringing the strength in his shoulders to her attention. Again. "Light sleeper. I heard the door close and got up to investigate."

"Sorry. I didn't mean to wake anybody else."

"I don't think you did. I'm surprised I heard it—Will must've been between snores."

She smiled in the dark. "We've got a good team here. Enthusiastic. Excited about the job."

"And what about you?"

"It's what I do." No way was she going to confide in him, if that's where his question was going. The last thing she needed was for her partner to have as little confidence in her ability as she did herself at the moment.

"How long have you been in?"

"What, CLEU? Four years. I went into the LAPD right out of college, then got tapped two years later."

"Your family happy about you being in police work?"

In a word, no. But that was none of his business. "My mother worries. My dad's military, so he knows the risks. We don't talk about it much." Understatement of the year. "What about you?"

Cooper stirred, and his loosely clasped hands tightened, then relaxed, as if he'd told himself to do so. "I was a foster kid. Never stayed too long in any one place, so it's hard to know who to call 'Mom and Dad.' At least I'm not making anyone worry."

It also meant he had no one to care. Joanna could hardly imagine a life so solitary. Her family drove her crazy sometimes—her dad had two brothers, and they'd had sons, and all the testosterone at Thanksgiving was enough to make a woman want to join a convent—but she still felt as though she was a part of something. And yeah, her dad didn't think much of any woman's abilities, but she still loved him. Still tried to please him, to make him smile the way he did at the triumphs of her cousins every time they scored on the stock market or caught a long pass.

"No siblings?" she asked at last. "Cousins? Grandparents?"

He shrugged. "My little sister and I were separated when I was twelve, because I was a problem kid. She was easy to place, but I wasn't. We keep in touch. She's married and has a new baby, up in Portland. I haven't met the baby yet."

"So you do have someone to worry about you."

"Not really. She knows I'm a cop, but she thinks I'm directing traffic and handing out parking tickets. She doesn't know about CLEU, and that's fine with me. They're my real family, anyway."

When he didn't elaborate, Joanna asked, "Your real family?"

"Yeah." He got up. "If you're going to feel all right tomorrow, you should get some sleep."

"I was trying. I finally gave up and came outside."

"I don't sleep real well the first night in a new place, either."

"Oh, it's not that. I was—" She stopped, before she gave herself away.

"What?" When she didn't answer, he strolled over to where she sat on the retaining wall and dropped down beside her. "It's not because of Tom Semple, is it?"

Well, crap. Why couldn't he be like the usual undercover cop and exchange some pleasantries, grunt and go back to bed, to snore uninterrupted until daybreak? Why did he have to be so perceptive, out here in the dark?

Not only that, heat radiated off his bare skin in the cool night air, warming her entire right side. Sleeping with him would be like curling up next to a furnace.

And where had *that* come from?

"Joanna?" he persisted when she didn't answer—too busy recoiling from the dangerous turn her thoughts had taken.

"Maybe," she admitted. "I'm weirded out by it, that's all. I don't like it."

He nodded. "You're not alone. You can bet I'll be

paying close attention in that class on Monday. There has to be something we're missing. A guy can't just walk up to a woman, touch her on the shoulder and turn her into a love-bot, just like that."

"Thanks a lot."

"You know what I mean. What did it feel like?"

She turned a little to stare at him. "What did what feel like?" Being touched? Being a love-bot? What?

"When he touched you the first time. Did he put the Vulcan pinch on you to cut off the circulation to your brain? Did you feel anything?"

Joanna tried to think, but it was difficult when he was sitting so close that his bare arm brushed hers. So, okay, he was talking about the case, but he was also talking about another man touching her, and that was getting a little bit personal, thank you very much.

With her left hand, she reached back and touched her right shoulder tendon. "He touched this tendon, here. That's all. No Vulcan pinch, nothing."

"What, right here?"

He ran one finger along the tendon from her shoulder to her neck, and she shivered. "Yes. That one."

"And then what?"

"And then nothing. He invited me over to his table and I went, because he seemed so nice."

"You remember what you said, but you still can't recall details."

"Not clearly. Not his face. It's fuzzy, like when you dream about something and it starts to fade." What was not fading here was the sensation of his finger running over her skin. It was setting up echoes inside her, the way a stone thrown into a pool sets up a series of rings, radiating outward from the central point of impact.

This was not good.

Or maybe it was a side effect of the Rules. Maybe if Cooper touched her again and suggested they go into the house and find somewhere more comfortable, she'd follow him like a zoned-out little puppy.

No. No fricking way.

"I'm going to bed," she said abruptly, and fled before he could say another word.

IN THE MORNING Cooper could almost believe he'd dreamed that conversation in the dark, if it hadn't been for the fact that kick-butt Joanna MacPherson was as skittish as a teenager on her first date. The question was, had it been that she'd confided in him after their disastrous beginning, or was it because he'd touched her?

He'd felt her shiver. He was no dummy where women were concerned—he knew as well as she did that their attraction hadn't gone away just because it was outside their professional boundaries right now. Or because she chose to ignore it.

What had made him run a finger along her skin when he knew she was uncomfortable sitting next to him? Why was he pushing her? Just how badly did he want a broken tibia?

Not that she looked ready to break anything at the moment. When she thought no one was paying attention, a distressed, haunted expression would pinch the corners of her eyes and turn down those pretty lips. Lips like that should be laughing or teasing or saying things to inflame a man's passion. They shouldn't be on the point of trembling.

Will came out of the bedroom with a backpack slung over one shoulder. "If you were serious about taking today off, I'm going to head up to San Francisco and get some stuff from my apartment. I wasn't sure how long this detail was going to be, so I packed pretty light."

Cooper nodded. "No problem. The Rules class starts at nine tomorrow, so as long as you're here around eight to wire me up, we're good."

Will nodded and loped down the front steps, heading for the gray Ford truck parked in front of the neighbor's house.

"What about you?" he called to Leah, who was busy typing in the comm room.

"I have family here in Santa Rita," she said. "I've got a note in my e-mail from my aunt, inviting me over for a barbecue. I'll probably head out in about an hour."

Which left him and Joanna, footloose and fancy-free for a whole day. Kellan and Linn had left on their honeymoon to Utah by now. He could give Danny a call and see whether he'd managed to escape the third bridesmaid and find someone more appealing to spend the weekend with. Or he could drive the eighty miles north to San Francisco and chill for the day in his condo. But that would leave Joanna on her own in a strange town, half a state away from her home in L.A.

If it had been him in that position, he'd appreciate a fellow investigator hanging out with him. But with women, who knew?

Leah departed around eleven, so he took her place in front of the big screen and cleaned up some e-mail. A few minutes later, he heard Joanna moving around in the kitchen, the clink of the coffee carafe on a mug and the rustle of the bag of bagels that Leah had picked up before any of them woke.

"Where is everyone?" Joanna wandered into the comm room, nibbling on an untoasted bagel slathered in cream cheese.

Cooper told her. "I could go back to my place, but I thought that since you aren't from around here, you might like to see the sights. And get acclimated."

"And these sights would be…?"

With a shrug, he said, "This is a college town. A beach town. So you can drink your double nonfat extra-hot latte, rent a surfboard, have a tofu burrito for lunch and see an independent movie, all in the same day. Take your pick."

"Or I could get on the 'net, spend the day researching these damn Rules and then go downtown and 'acclimate' myself."

"You could," he allowed. "But I think you should take a day to disengage. Last night upset you. It might be good to think about something else."

"How would you know what upsets me?"

Broken bones loomed in his future, but he replied anyway. "I don't. But sleeplessness and your expression when you think people aren't looking are pretty good indications. Come on, Joanna." He held up a hand when she straightened and her consumption of the bagel became downright savage. "You don't have to be superwoman around here. Save the warrior persona for the suspects. I need you to be real."

The last bite of the bagel went down sideways and she coughed, which let him get another word in.

"Yeah, we didn't expect what happened last night. Yeah, it's upsetting—for all of us, not just you. But we have to take a step back from that and gain some equilibrium here, so that we're operating on facts, not emotion."

"I don't operate on emotion," she managed to rasp between coughing fits.

"That's good. Then you'll agree with me that we need to disengage for today. Ever done any sailing?"

"Sailing."

"Yeah, like on a boat."

"I know what sailing is. No, I haven't. And I don't plan to start today. It's one thing to spend my working hours taking orders from you. The thought of having to swab decks in my leisure time does not appeal."

Her glare was so poisonous and her expectations so ludicrous that he had to laugh. "I promise. No swabbing. All you have to do is sit in the stern and pull on a rope once in a while. That's it."

She didn't look convinced. In fact, she looked ready to turn and walk out.

"And the best part is, we'll be completely off the grid. No calls, no people, no criminals, no case. Just the sky and the ocean and the wind."

"You'll probably make us capsize."

"Nope. Remember UC Santa Rita's reputation? The four *S*s—surfing, scuba, sailing—and science."

"What does that have to do with anything?" she asked.

"I'm an alum, which means I can take out any of the sailboats in the summer when there aren't any classes. Come on. What do you say?"

She looked as though he'd offered her a discount on a root canal. "What can I say? I sit in the house by myself or I go sailing with you. Be still, my foolish heart."

There was one good thing about it, he thought as they gathered their things. Since she didn't know how to operate sails and rudder, he had a hundred percent chance of making it back to shore alive.

7

COOPER TURNED THE BOAT one more degree to the right—so was that port or starboard?—and the sail bellied out as the breeze filled it. Sprawled on the wide bench seat in the stern, Joanna grabbed for the nearest rail as the deck tilted and they picked up speed.

Cooper let out a whoop and took a firmer grip on the tiller. He did something with the ropes in his left hand—he called them "sheets" for reasons that Joanna couldn't fathom—that made the boat go even faster.

What was it with guys and speed, anyway? Whether it was careening around street corners on two wheels, or galloping across Junipero Bay with nothing between them and the sharks except a fragile shell of a hull, men seemed to think you weren't having fun unless you were racing flat out.

"Isn't this great?" he hollered over his shoulder. "What a perfect day."

It was a lucky thing she didn't get seasick.

Any woman but herself would think it really was a perfect day. The man clearly knew what he was doing, the sun was brilliant but not too hot and they were completely cut off from everything but themselves.

Which, of course, was the underlying cause of her unhappy state of mind.

What had she been thinking to agree to this? She was now half a mile from shore, surrounded by water and trapped on a sixteen-foot boat with the one man who could destroy a night's sleep with a single touch.

He seemed blissfully unaware of it, but it was eating her up. He had touched her in the same way Tom Semple had, and her body had reacted the way a match did on sandpaper—it had ignited. What did these Rules do to a woman, anyway? Was she no longer in control of her physical responses? Did he just have to touch her shoulder and she turned into a—what had Cooper called it—a love-bot?

No. Absolutely not.

She had to be in control, still. She decided who attracted her and whom she allowed to touch her. Not any random guy off the street.

But how to find out for sure?

Again, her gaze fell on Cooper, now squinting happily into the distance from under the bill of his ball cap. He wore the same old jeans he'd had on last night, and from where she sat, she observed that they hugged his butt as nicely as they did his thighs. Very nicely indeed. He'd pulled off his windbreaker as soon as they'd cleared the harbor, and wore a white collared T-shirt that emphasized the muscles in his arms as they flexed and tightened with every movement of ropes and rudder.

Hmm.

He'd made it plain he was attracted to her, even

though she'd done everything in her power to beat him back and put him in his place. And except for that one touch last night, she'd succeeded.

Mostly. He was like a wolf in the forest, pacing back and forth just beyond the light of the campfire, watching her. He'd admitted it, hadn't he? Something about her expression looking unhappy when she thought no one noticed.

He'd given himself away there.

So what would happen if she invited him to stop looking? Here they were, cut off from everything, outside the Rules. Just two people out on the bay where no one could see them unless they happened to sail past within twenty feet.

She needed to find out if she still had normal responses to a man. She needed to know she was not being controlled by the Rules, that she hadn't been messed up in some fundamental way.

What happened on the boat stayed on the boat, right?

The wind dropped off and the bow dipped a little as their speed slowed. The deck tilted back down until it was nearly level, and Cooper trimmed the sails. Jo relaxed into the corner and lifted both legs up onto the long bench seat. Her short denim skirt rode up a couple of inches. Out of the corner of her eye, she saw Cooper's attention catch and hold. Languidly, as though enjoying the warmth of the sun, she pulled off her long-sleeved shirt, revealing the moss-green cotton cami with its scooped neckline and spaghetti straps underneath. She stretched like a cat, her arms along the top of the seat cushions, arching her back and thrusting her breasts into prominence.

Any man in his right mind would get the message.

Cooper cinched the mainsail's sheet down so that the sail luffed aimlessly in the wind. "I guess we're out far enough," he said. "We can drift for a while without running into anything."

Since land was a green smudge in the distance and the nearest sail was a crescent the size of her fingernail on the horizon, Joanna figured they probably could. Whether there was enough time to seduce him remained to be seen. She hadn't done this in a while. In fact, come to think of it, she hadn't ever done it. Most of the men she dated—including the late unlamented Michael Dunn—were so straightforward about what they wanted that she'd never had to seduce anybody. Was there a right way to go about it? She didn't know. She'd just have to go with her gut, the way she did in investigations, and see what happened.

"Not feeling sick or anything?" Cooper sat on the bench close to her feet, so she turned a little, lifting one knee. If he chose, he could get a view up the length of her thigh under the skirt.

"No," she replied. "Either I'm immune or it's not very rough out here."

"Probably a combination of both. Good thing. It'd take a lot of the pleasure out of the day if I had to keep holding your head over the rail."

She grinned at the image, and her gaze caught on his.

"You should do that more often."

"Do what?"

"Smile. I think it's the first time I've seen it since I met you."

Okay, so that wasn't very seductive, but she'd get him there. She allowed the smile to curve her lips, and kept them soft enough to invite a kiss. But he wouldn't be kissing anybody two cushions away. Time to rethink that strategy.

She swiveled and tucked her legs underneath her, turning toward him as she relaxed against the seat back, one wrist dangling along the top. To the best of her knowledge, her body language said, "Come closer," but he didn't.

Maybe she'd been a little too forceful in the "back off" body language yesterday. Maybe she needed to reinforce this with verbal cues.

Maybe she needed to quit overthinking the whole situation and try something completely radical—like enjoying his company. What a concept.

He stretched out his legs and slouched on the cushions. "This is the life. Thanks for coming with me."

"I had my doubts," she admitted. "I've never been exposed much to boats."

"I thought you were a military brat."

"I am, but that doesn't mean—" She stopped. "Where did you hear that?"

"You told me. Last night. Your mom worries about you, but your dad's military, so he knows the risks."

"Oh, yeah." For a moment there, she thought he might have read her personnel file. Scary thought. "He's navy, but that doesn't mean us kids spent much time on the ships. Besides, there's a big difference between a destroyer and this little thing."

"This little thing is easier to steer."

She did not want to talk about steering boats. She wanted to steer the conversation to sex. Or better yet, to stop conversing at all.

But how to get there from here outside of simply climbing into his lap and kissing him senseless?

Because the longer she sat this close to him, the more sensitive she became to every nuance of his breathing, his movements, even the way his hair stirred on the nape of his neck. She might tell herself she was looking for a sign, watching for some signal of interest, but the truth was, she just liked looking at him. He was tall and smart and sexy as all hell—and she appreciated that in a man.

Let's be honest, here, Joanna. You just plain want the guy and you're mad because he moved on you yesterday before you were ready. Before you could control the situation.

And yes, she needed to resolve this Rules thing, but that was in addition to a few other recently dormant needs that were clamoring to be satisfied.

"Something bothering you, Joanna?" Cooper extended his arm along the back of the seat cushion, his fingers a scant inch from her wrist.

Yes. You bother me. You, with your capable body and your hazel eyes and your little-boy grin. "What makes you say that?"

He pulled off his cap and ran a careless hand through his hair. The breeze did the rest, tousling it in a way that would be disastrous on many men, but that just made him look loose and uninhibited.

Yeah, you wish.

"I don't know. You've been kinda quiet and thoughtful since yesterday. I know the Rules are bugging you, and before that I was bugging you. I just wanted to make sure we were okay before we jump into this case with both feet tomorrow."

"I thought we'd left the case onshore for today."

He grinned, and damn if a big old dimple didn't carve itself into his cheek next to his mouth. It just wasn't fair.

"We did. I was just checking."

There just wasn't a way to bring this up gracefully. She couldn't just come out and say, "Cooper, I need to climb into your lap and kiss you senseless to make sure all my neurons are firing correctly. Do you mind?"

Or maybe she could.

"You can tell me something." Her heart began to pound, the way it did when a big case was about to go down.

"Sure. What?"

"When we danced at that wedding yesterday, what were you thinking?"

His gaze became very focused, very intent. "Why do you ask?"

"Because I want to know."

"Before or after I groped you?"

Was he looking for another fight? Or was he just using words to stave off what was about to happen? "Before."

"I think you know."

"Tell me."

"Why? So you can have me written up for harassment? I didn't know you were a cop at that point, Joanna."

"I know. I didn't know you were one, either. All I knew was that something was happening." Her gaze dropped to his mouth, for about the fifteenth time that day. "Something good."

Heat kindled in his eyes, but, ever the professional, darn him, he didn't move. "So you admit we had chemistry."

"Have. Have chemistry."

The temperature rose another degree. She closed the gap along the cushion backs and ran her fingers over his hand.

"What are you telling me?" His voice had gone a little rough.

"I think you know."

"And I think you know it's not going to happen as long as we're working together."

Now he chose to be honorable? Honestly. Men.

"We're not working right now."

"You're splitting hairs." But even as he spoke, his gaze dropped even lower, to her collarbone, to her chest…to her nipples under the camisole, which had begun to ache with frustrated desire. Which meant they were probably poking at the fabric and making her thoughts as easy to read as a headline in the paper.

The fact that she wasn't wearing a bra seemed to detonate in his head.

"You're not playing fair," he whispered.

She had him.

Joanna wasn't sure who moved first, but in the next second she wrapped her arms around his neck and he pushed her back against the cushions, one hand around her waist and the other cradling her head. And then his mouth came down on hers and everything she'd been imagining for the past twenty-four hours came true in one heart-stopping moment.

Oh, man, did he know how to kiss. His lips teased and nibbled and tempted, hot and soft at the same time. His tongue met hers, sliding the length of it, promising and drawing back, telling her in the most primitive and unmistakable way that he had a lot more to offer if she'd allow it.

A sound came from deep in her throat, acknowledging that she'd like nothing more than to allow it.

He broke the kiss and left her gasping for breath as his mouth moved along her jawline, exploring the textures of her skin. Helplessly, her head fell back, giving him access to the hollow under her ear, the contours of her neck, the ridge of her collarbone. With his thumb, he moved one spaghetti strap off her shoulder and the other seemed to fall off by itself, leaving her bared to the slow tease of his tongue.

"Come here," he said, and rolled to a sitting position with her astride his lap, just as she'd wanted for the last half hour.

Cooper tilted his head back. "Confession time."

"Mmm?" He smelled so good. Some light cologne and salt and clean cotton, all intensified by the warmth of the sun and the rising heat between them. She nuzzled the soft spot under his ear, breathing in.

"I've wanted this since I saw you at the wedding, partner or not."

"In that case, I have a confession, too."

He slid both hands around her waist, under the camisole. "Do you, now?"

"It's your fault for coming out last night with no shirt on. I was just managing to hold it all together and then you went and did that."

"I didn't know it was you. If I had, maybe I'd've come out in just my boxers."

She smothered a smile in the side of his neck. "I'm shocked, Investigator."

"You ain't seen nothing yet."

He turned his head and captured her lips again. At the same time, he seated her more firmly in his lap.

"Oh, my," she whispered against his mouth.

"Oh, yes. This is what you get when you don't wear a bra."

"Remind me to do it more often," she breathed.

Her skirt had ridden up to the top of her thighs, leaving them bare to the caress of his hands. His erection pressed against her with a heat and hardness she could feel through a layer of denim and the silk of her underwear.

Who wears turquoise silk underpants on an afternoon sail? You're so transparent, Joanna MacPherson.

Maybe. But she was a woman on a mission. While frissons of pleasure chased themselves over her skin as he touched her thighs and slid his hands up under her skirt to curve around her derriere, somewhere in the back of her mind, she took note of each response.

That's normal. His hands there aren't doing anything to control me. When he touches me there, I feel nothing but pleasure. It's all right. I'm not a love-bot. I'm okay.

Cooper stroked upward from thigh to waist once more. "I hope you don't have strong feelings about indecent exposure."

She chuckled, a sound filled with the knowledge of what he intended to do. "I don't suppose we're in international waters yet?"

"No." Slowly, his hands slid up her ribs, taking the hem of the camisole with them.

"Where's my sunblock?"

His palms lay flat against her skin, thumbs resting just under the lower curve of her breasts. Her breathing flattened out with anticipation, and she bit her lip to stop herself from begging him to touch her.

"No sunblock," he said firmly. "That's just one more thing covering you."

"Please." The word escaped her on a whisper.

"Tell me what you want."

"You know what I want."

"But I want to hear you say it."

"Take my top off," she said raggedly. "Lick me. Suck me. I want to feel your mouth on me."

With a groan, he pulled her camisole up over her head and tossed it aside. She felt the sun strike flesh where it didn't normally go, and the ocean breeze caressed her skin. But the sun wasn't nearly as hot as Cooper's eyes, or the touch of the breeze nearly as exciting as that of his mouth on her at last.

She shivered as he kissed a hot, damp trail into her cleavage. He cupped her flesh in both hands, and murmured with husky satisfaction, burying his face in the valley between her breasts and kissing his way back up again. He traced sensual circles with his tongue, narrowing in on her nipples in an unhurried way that drove her—type A personality that she was—crazy with frustration and arousal.

Oh, yes, this was normal. There were no damned Rules operating here.

And then at last he took her nipple into his mouth, nibbling and licking, his tongue hot and agile on the sensitive, aching nub.

"Oh, that's good," she gasped.

His big hands cupped her, shaping and drinking her in through touch as his mouth drove her mad. When he finally released her, it was just to capture her mouth again while he skimmed her underwear off and tossed it to join her camisole. At least when the Coast Guard motored up to arrest them, she'd still have her skirt on.

"Your turn," she said, and pulled his shirt out of the waistband of his jeans and over his head.

He pulled her to him so that her breasts flattened against his bare chest, and she looped her arms around his neck as she kissed him.

"Your skin feels good on mine," he murmured, his hands moving across her back. "So soft."

The mat of hair on his chest softly abraded the sensitive places where his mouth had been. Teased. Tickled. Was there nothing about this man that didn't turn her on? For Pete's sake, she even liked his feet, and how crazy was that?

If nothing else, that proved she wasn't a love-bot.

She sat back and unfastened the button of his jeans, then the zipper. "These have to go before you burst out of them."

He grinned at her, all male and sure of himself. "Can't wait, huh?"

"Maybe." She leaned in and kissed him. "We'll see who lasts the longest."

He toed off his deck shoes and stripped both boxers and jeans off in one lithe movement. "It won't be me. I am so into you right now that one touch could send me."

She tsked, shaking her head. "Ladies first."

"Always." He snagged his jeans and extracted a small foil packet from his wallet. After sheathing himself, he grabbed her around the waist and hauled her back into his lap. "Now, where were we?"

"Ladies were first," she said, snugging down onto the length of his erection. She was so wet, so ready for him she could hardly bear it. Every cell in her body called out for his, demanding fulfillment.

As she leaned forward to impale herself on his rigid length, he sucked a nipple into his mouth. Both hands fondled her while she raised up a little and hovered over the tip of his penis. His hips lifted toward her and she lowered herself slowly onto him.

With a long moan of satisfaction, she savored the way he filled her, stretched her, and finally hilted himself completely inside her.

"Cooper," she sighed. "You feel so good."

His thighs began to quiver, as if he were holding himself back from thrusting like a madman. Was he allowing her to control the pace? He'd put her on top right away, so he must be.

How divine. Well, she could be just as considerate.

She began to move up and down on him. His head fell back, and his eyelids drooped as he took her in, watching the way her breasts bounced with each stroke as if it were the only thing his world contained.

She discovered she liked that. She liked being his sole focus, even out here where wind and water could interrupt them at any second. For him, the world had fallen away and she was obviously the only thing in it.

He slipped a hand between their bodies and found her clitoris, slick and creamy wet with the evidence of her need. He began to stroke her, and she made another discovery. She was going to have to eat her words.

His fingers felt glorious. So slippery. Such pleasure. How could she contain it? Up and down and around and oh—

Oh—

Joanna's body convulsed around his clever fingers and marvelous cock and exploded into a million sparkles of red sunlight.

He swore and grabbed her hips, thrusting into her savagely and she screamed with pleasure and he let go of his control.

His hips flexed again and again and again—

Oh—

He cried out and came hard inside her and she laughed with the triumph and sweetness of it.

They fell sideways on the bench seat, knocking cushions to the floor, and lay gasping, still buried deep in each other's bodies. Cooper wrapped his arms around her and she felt the last remaining shudders of his satisfaction as she flattened her hands against his beautiful rear end.

After long minutes she slowly became aware of the slap of the waves against the hull. The cry of seagulls wheeling overhead.

The slap of waves against the hull. Big waves.

Joanna raised her head. "Cooper?"

"Mmm?"

"Is that an engine?"

"Mmm."

She looked over the rail. "Cooper!"

The Coast Guard cutter's engine shifted gears with a guttural growl as it slowed to make its second pass.

8

144 Vista Mar
Santa Rita, California
16:45 hours

THE SAFE HOUSE was empty when they arrived, for which Cooper was thankful. He could use an hour or two of downtime to recover from the amazing highs and lows of this afternoon.

The low, of course, being the fact that they'd been busted by the Coast Guard for making out in a boat, as though they'd been teenagers parked at Lovers' Lane.

It had been kind of funny, though.

Joanna had rolled to the floor with a squeak of dismay, yanking on her clothes in a frenzy. He'd just managed to jam his feet into his jeans and get them done up before the agent hailed them. It hadn't taken much more than a wave of his shield and an assurance that they were fine, they'd just fallen asleep, to make the Guard motor off on more interesting business.

By this time Joanna was in fits of giggles, and she'd sputtered over like a boiling kettle off and on all the way back here.

At least a sense of humor was finding its way to the

surface, not to mention this amazingly sensual hellcat who had made him yell with sheer pleasure not two hours ago. His body throbbed in appreciation at the memory. She kept both bottled up under a veneer of "career cop," which he supposed was a defense mechanism. It was a sad fact that a woman's sexuality was more of a liability in this job than an asset.

And he had catalogued her assets pretty thoroughly this afternoon. The question was, would he ever get a chance to do it again? And if so, how soon?

His chances looked pretty good. Instead of a frown of concentration or disapproval, which had depended on whether she was in the comm room or in a room with him in it, she now wore a soft smile. Her body had that languid, sensual looseness some women got after they'd been completely satisfied, making her hips swing a little more and her hands linger a little longer when she reached out to touch something. And did her lips look a little swollen, still?

He needed to be careful not to stare at her too much, or Will and Leah would figure out that there was something going on between the two of them. In fact, he needed to get his head straight on exactly what *was* going on between them.

Originally he'd envisioned one hot night between two strangers, with a kiss goodbye in the morning and a promise to call. Or not, depending on how they felt. But now…everything was different. She'd let her anger and her inhibitions and even her principles go—and so had he. This was a delicate situation that called for discretion and care. The last thing either of them needed was to be written up for inappropriate behavior. He had no intention of making this the final undercover op of his career.

He tapped on the door of the room she shared with Leah.

"Come in." Joanna sat cross-legged on the bed with her cell phone to her ear.

"You know, I've been thinking—"

"This isn't a good time, Cooper."

"But I think we need to—"

"Hey, Carleen?" Her attention switched from him to her call. "Yeah, it's me."

He backed out of the room and closed the door behind him. So much for that plan. Frowning, he walked into the living room and saw Will pulling up at the curb outside. No doubt Leah would be showing up any minute, too. They couldn't have driven down in the morning? Any hopes he'd had of a replay of this afternoon in the comfort of a real bed evaporated in a sizzle of disappointment.

There was no opportunity to get Joanna alone after that. The four of them went to dinner at a seafood place on the pier, and because they were in public, no one brought up the Rules or even the fact that they were state investigators. They were simply four coworkers out for a plate of crab legs and some laughs.

The crab legs were great. But Cooper didn't feel so much like laughing. No until he talked to Joanna. They had to get this—experience? Relationship? One time event?—clarified before they launched full bore into the investigation, because he could guarantee there wouldn't be a whole lot of time or privacy for talking once they got started.

Leah had one too many margaritas, so Joanna helped her into the car, and afterward into the house and down the hall to their room. Cooper killed time checking his e-mail, wandering out into the kitchen, then down the hall to where the women's door was closed, with a crack of light showing under it.

Was she just going to go to bed? Didn't women have a biological need to talk things over with a man after they'd had sex? Wasn't the "where do we go from here" conversation the number one male fear—with good reason?

Then how come he couldn't pin her down long enough to have the damn conversation? Not that he was fooling himself that either of them wanted a relationship. He just wanted to know that she was happy, that she was okay with what they'd done and, above all, that she wasn't going to let it jeopardize the job.

At ten-thirty he heard the water running in the en suite shower that had been built into her and Leah's room. At ten forty-five the crack of light under the door went out.

Well, crap.

"Got something on your mind?" Will passed him in the hall on his way to the kitchen.

"What makes you say that?"

Will shrugged. "You've been pacing around here since we got back from dinner. Bad news in e-mail?"

Cooper shook his head. "No, nothing like that. I'm just—" he thought fast "—strategizing. Moving around helps me think."

Someday, Will would make a fine investigator. He didn't even question his temporary senior officer. "I figured it might be something like that. Well, I'm turning in, too. See you in the morning."

Cooper nodded and strolled into the comm room, as though he'd forgotten something.

He slouched in the chair in front of the monitoring deck. How ridiculous was this situation, anyway? He wanted to exchange a few sentences with another consenting adult, that was all. And yet it was turning out to be frustratingly impossible. Will and Leah made chaperones as effective as any army of teachers at a high-school dance. They could talk, sure, out on the patio. But he wanted more than that. If he wanted to taste Joanna's mouth again, or better yet, the delights of that lithe body, he was going to have to get creative.

But getting creative required two people to be in on the plan, and that closed bedroom door didn't look very positive. Maybe she was upset with herself and was too proud to show it in front of him and the others. Maybe she'd had second thoughts and didn't want to tell him to get lost. Maybe it was simply that she'd chosen to focus on the investigation now, and their day off was over.

Which, of course, was exactly what she should do. And what he should do, too. The problem was, he couldn't seem to do it.

This was a first. He was the guy who kept his relationships at a distance. Nothing came before the job and his brothers in law enforcement. If Kellan or Danny needed something—whether it was a ride to the office from the car dealership or an informal workout for his psych degree with a man who needed to talk—he was the go-to guy. He'd turn to his date, explain the situation, and then walk away without a backward glance.

Of course, your average woman had a hard time seeing this point of view. But the average woman he might date probably had a family to fall back on. If he let down his brothers in law enforcement, who would he fall back on?

Nobody. So, setting priorities was easy for him. Walking away without hurting anyone had become somewhat of an art form.

He had had a lot of practice at being the one who was left behind, though. And now that he was in that position, he wasn't sure he liked it much.

His gaze fell on one of the two phones on the console. The landline was for CLEU business and the cell sitting upright in its charger was the "hot number," or the unit a suspect could call to get an officer who was working undercover and playing the role of drug dealer or fence or whatever. The hot number was monitored by Leah's bank of equipment. The landline was not.

Before he had too much time to think about what this might mean, Cooper picked up the landline. Joanna's cell number was in her file. Her cell was probably in her handbag, but he had a fifty-fifty chance she had it set to vibrate instead of ring, and he could say what he needed to say without Leah overhearing.

"You've reached Joanna MacPherson," her recorded voice informed him in a crisp, businesslike tone. "Please leave a message and I'll get back to you."

"Joanna, it's Cooper," he said quietly. "I wanted to tell you that I had a good time today. And that you are an amazing woman. I know we're not going to have much privacy around here, but at some point I want to talk. Alone. We could meet out on the patio. Or somewhere else." He paused. Should he tell her what he really wanted? Should he remind her about the incredible pleasure they'd shared and say how much he wanted it again? Maybe not. Who knew where she'd be when she got the message? "Well, wish me luck tomorrow. See you in the morning."

He hung up. Okay, so the sign-off had been a little lame. But at least she'd know he wanted to see her in a nonofficial capacity. That he wasn't the one walking away.

What she didn't know was that this was the first time he could say that—and mean it.

9

West Side Community Center, Room #254
10:25 hours

"DEEP DOWN, every woman wants to be seduced."

Cooper glanced around the classroom as twenty-four men of ages from anywhere between 21 and 55 bent to their workbooks as if this were the secret to the meaning of life. At the front of the room, the instructor, who wore a plastic name tag with Richard Benton written on it in black felt pen, called up the first slide of his presentation on a PC connected to a projector, and looked at each man in turn.

From his seat at the back, Cooper returned his gaze with bland interest.

"The reason you're here this morning is because each of you has struck out with women. Maybe it's your approach. Maybe it's your looks. Maybe you're searching in the wrong places. No matter what the reason, you're here because you need help and you've heard about the workshop through word of mouth. For obvious reasons, we don't advertise, and no women are enrolled in our seminars. The Rules of Seduction are for men only."

A guy with a bad comb-over and an iPod in his pocket where plastic protectors had been in the eighties raised his hand. "Why aren't women in these classes? Wouldn't we be better off if they were seducing us, too?"

Benton smiled. "They will be seducing you. But you can't hit a home run unless someone gives you a bat, can you? The Rules are your bat."

A lawyer type with natty tortoiseshell glasses frowned. "That sounds kinda violent. I'm not into that. I just want to get laid."

"I was speaking in a metaphorical sense." The instructor touched a key and the slide changed to a stock photo of a typical bar scene. His students studied the shot. "Let me show you what I mean. What do you see here?"

"A bunch of people having a good time," the lawyer said. "Bars never look like that when I'm there."

"It all depends on your perception. By tomorrow afternoon, you'll have learned not only the Rules, but also the skills and behaviors that go with them that will change your perception of this picture entirely. There are only three Rules, but the skills are an infinitely flexible framework that can change your life."

"Can you be more specific?" Cooper figured it was high time he got engaged in the classroom discussion. Not enough to stand out, but enough to assure anyone that he was just as clueless about women as they were.

"Absolutely." Benton pressed the key and the slide changed again. Everyone in the room sat up, their attention riveted to the screen.

"As you can see, the naked female body is a beautiful thing. This young lady's name is Cherise, and I'm showing her nude body to you so you can get used to it before you see her in person. I don't want you distracted from our exercises because you're speculating about what's under her clothes."

"What?" The lawyer loosened his tie, as though he were already sweating. "The syllabus didn't say anything about naked women."

"The class includes several hands-on exercises between yourselves, Cherise and other classroom assistants, where your attention will be focused on physical responses. Rest assured, all the ladies are bonded and insured and have done at least twenty workshops. They'll put you completely at your ease."

"Is Cherise single?" the iPod guy wanted to know.

"She is not."

The guy shrugged. "Worth a try."

"So." The instructor indicated Cherise's nude form, and tapped the keyboard so that a series of glowing lines were superimposed upon it. "Let's begin. The first Rule is, *Attraction is the first phase of the biological imperative to procreate. It is not an involuntary response.*"

"What do you mean?" A guy in a Ramones T-shirt looked puzzled. "Attraction is spontaneous. You can't control it. And it's different with every guy. What does it for me won't attract him." He jerked a thumb toward the lawyer. "Or him." The thumb pointed in Cooper's direction.

"I'm not talking about your attraction to a woman. I'm talking about hers to you once you single her out. Remember our bar scene a few minutes ago? You see a woman, you're attracted to her, you go up and talk to her."

"*You* might." iPod guy slid down a few inches in his chair. "Too risky for me."

"That's why you're here," Benton said patiently, then turned back to his computer. "This slide demonstrates the energy meridians of the body. The Rules of Seduction tell us that a reciprocal attraction can be generated in a woman by a combination of verbal cues and stimulation of these meridians at certain points."

"I don't believe it." The lawyer crossed his arms over his chest.

"Sounds too yoga for me," a guy in a flannel shirt agreed, with a sideways glance at the door. Maybe he was wondering whether he could get his fifteen hundred bucks back. "What the hell's a meridian?"

"These yellow lines of energy. For instance." With a laser pointer, the instructor tracked a glowing path from the model's wrist, up her arm, to her breast, where he circled the nipple. That pulled Flannel Guy's attention off the door and back to the screen.

"Say you're sitting at a bar. Step one, you're attracted. Step two, you approach a woman. Step three, you engage her in conversation."

"Step four, she says 'Kiss off, freak' and walks away," said iPod Guy.

"Step four," Benton corrected him, "you interrupt her instinctive default to caution by stimulating the meridian point on the underside of her wrist. Just a light touch will do it. This interrupts her response and allows you an opening in her defenses. At this point you employ the verbal cue to form a mental connection. With both physical and mental responses engaged, you bypass the walls, as it were, and move on to the metaphorical attack."

"What verbal cue? How do we know what that is?"

The lawyer was writing everything down in his workbook as though he were preparing a case.

"We'll get to that. For now, let me introduce Cherise and give you a demonstration."

A door opened at the rear of the room and Cherise walked in. She was a young Asian-American woman with the kind of body men paid to look at via online cameras. She wore skinny jeans and one of those glittery baby-doll tops all the women were wearing these days, with varying degrees of success. On Cherise it was an eye-popping thing of beauty, particularly since she wore no bra.

Cooper had a moment to wonder if he'd be able to lay charges here outside the scope of their investigation of assaults. Just what was going to happen now that they had a live woman in the room, regardless of whether she was bonded and insured?

Cherise perched on the edge of the table on which the projector sat, and the instructor sat next to her.

"Say I've just approached this attractive woman at Atlantis," he said. Cooper catalogued the fact that he knew the area. Interesting, for a workshop that moved all over the state. "I've just said hello. Now, watch."

Cherise's body language clearly said, "Back away, old guy, I'm looking for something better." Even her eyes showed a sort of pained disinterest, and one row over, Flannel Guy nodded with recognition, as if he'd seen that look more times than he cared to count.

The instructor slid his hand under Cherise's palm, as though he was going to shake her hand, and before she could pull away, his long, elegant fingers stroked the underside of her wrist. Her eyes locked on his in arrested curiosity, as though he'd told her something she hadn't known before, and under the sleek jersey of her top, her nipples hardened into nubs visible even at the back of the room.

Every man in the class leaned forward in his seat. Cooper's eyes narrowed. Was this what had happened to Joanna? He'd been behind her when Tom Semple had made his move, so he hadn't seen the signs of arousal. He'd been more concerned about her mental processes, and the fact that her danger was escalating even as he watched.

Besides, the only physical reactions he was interested in were the ones she had when she was alone with him.

"Do you ever feel like you did when you were a child, getting ready to jump off the diving board at the pool?" Benton asked Cherise in a low, intimate tone, still stroking her wrist.

"Oh, yeah," she said. "I always liked diving."

The instructor sat back and released her hand. Cherise sat back, too, and the visible evidence of sexual interest faded. One or two of the students exhaled audibly. Someone in the row by the window shifted uncomfortably in his seat.

"Let's walk through that step by step, and then we'll go into a deeper analysis of physiological responses," Benton told them. "Along with all the Rules, we'll learn the three meridian points in the upper body today, and the three in the lower body tomorrow. In between, i.e., tonight, you'll do some field work by going to a bar in pairs to test and observe what you've learned."

Cooper made another mental note. The team had

just had their happy hunting ground outlined for them. He'd huddle with them when class was over. Meantime, because of the transmitter he wore, Joanna would know as much about what would happen as he did, and this time they'd be much better prepared.

Richard Benton looked around, but there were no questions. "Now, then." A tap on the keyboard produced a slide featuring a drawing of a woman's wrist, much like those Cooper had seen in medical illustrations. "The easiest meridian to work with in a public situation is here, on the inner wrist. Even slight pressure at that point will stimulate and alter a woman's response to you. And how can you tell that it worked?"

The men looked at one another. iPod Guy raised a tentative hand, then lowered it again.

"Please." The instructor invited him to speak. "There are no social niceties here. Just tell us what you observed."

"Uh, her—" He glanced at Cherise in apology, and she smiled at him. "I don't know about anything else, but her um, nipples were, uh…"

"Exactly. That is the primary indicator that you have found the meridian point. The woman's nipples will involuntarily become erect. Then you know it's appropriate to say the verbal cue. Unless, of course, she's wearing a padded bra." The class chuckled. "Did anyone pick up on what the cue was?"

Silence.

"I don't get what swimming has to do with seduction," Cooper admitted aloud for all of them.

"Ah, but I didn't say anything about swimming. I used the words *feel, ready* and *diving. Feel* allows her to give herself permission to open up to me. *Ready* cues her state of mind. And *diving,* of course, indicates subliminally that I would like to perform oral sex on her, an act women love and which it's widely known they don't get as often as they'd like."

"Whoa," Flannel Guy said. "I didn't get any of that. I was trying to figure out if you were going to ask her for a swim date."

"It's not about asking for a date, gentlemen," the instructor said. "Remember the First Rule. It's about priming a woman to accept her attraction to you as a biological imperative. Once she does that, the field is open." He turned to Cherise, still perched on the edge of the table. "Thank you, my dear. See you during the next module."

With a smile, she slid off the table and walked to the door. Every man in the room watched those perfect, unsupported breasts jiggle every time she set her stiletto heels down.

Every man but one. The lawyer was still busy taking notes. Cooper smothered a smile. No wonder the poor guy couldn't get a date.

"I'VE GOT A HIT."

Joanna finished up a report and closed the online file, then looked over her shoulder at Leah. "That didn't take long. Good work."

Leah pushed a piece of paper toward her. "Central Coast General Hospital admitted an assault victim at three o'clock Saturday morning. Mid-twenties, single. Fits our profile. The other victims were in the same range."

"Did they release a name?"

"Yep." Leah's fingers flashed on the keys. "Here's her driver's license info, including a picture. I'll print it."

"Find the one you printed for Thomas Semple while you're at it, okay? I'll show it to her when I interview her, and see if it rings any bells."

"It might." Leah pulled a sheet of paper out of the color printer. "Look at this."

The woman's name was Tracey Bigelow. Five foot six, a hundred and thirty pounds, blue eyes, red hair.

Red hair?

Joanna's gaze narrowed on the woman's picture. *No. She doesn't look a bit like me. And she's three inches shorter.*

It simply wasn't rational to be afraid. There was hardly even a passing resemblance between them, and besides, poor Tracey Bigelow probably hadn't had the benefit of police self-defense training and ongoing kick-boxing classes.

Would that have done any good, with the state of mind—or lack thereof—she'd been in when Thomas Semple had led her to the door?

Joanna tucked both pictures in her handbag, grabbed the keys to the unmarked vehicle in the garage and headed out. With the help of the map in the glove compartment, she found the hospital in about twenty minutes, and the admitting desk directed her to Ms. Bigelow's room.

Fortunately, poor Tracey's eyes were closed when she halted next to the bed, so Joanna had a moment to school her features into something other than shock.

"Assault" was putting it mildly. Someone had worked her over but good, including giving her a black eye, a cut lip, a bruised temple and a number of finger-shaped bruises that extended down her neck and out of sight beneath the hospital gown.

The woman must have heard Joanna's slow intake of breath. Her eyes opened, and something that might have been the shadow of fear passed through them.

"Ms. Bigelow," Joanna said, flashing her shield, "I'm Joanna MacPherson with the California Law Enforcement Unit. I'm investigating a series of crimes against persons in this area. Do you feel well enough to answer a few questions?"

The woman's lips moved, but no sound came out. Joanna snagged a pitcher standing on a nearby table and poured her a glass of water, then helped her sit up in order to drink it.

"I don't know what I can tell you." The words came slowly, stumbling past the cut and swollen lip.

Joanna pulled up a chair upholstered in yellow vinyl. "Do you remember anything about the assault? Or who did it?"

"I don't know his name."

With her notebook at the ready, Joanna decided to take this slow and steady. "Were you abducted or robbed?"

A slow shake of the head. "I went to a club. Koko. Here."

"Club Koko? I was there Saturday night. Were you, as well?"

The woman shook her head. "Friday night-Saturday morning. I danced with some people, and then he came. Sat at my table. Must've looked okay. I think I left with him."

"You think?"

"Can't remember very well."

This was beginning to sound very familiar. "Do you remember if he touched you when he sat with you?"

Her brow furrowed. "Touched?"

Joanna nodded. "Maybe he ran a finger along your shoulder, here?" She twisted a little and demonstrated. "Or somewhere else?"

A glimmer of light came into the dull eyes. "I think so. How do you know?"

"Because it happened to me Saturday night. A guy came up to my table, touched me like I just showed you, and before I knew it, I was Zombie Girl. Everything he said seemed to make perfect sense, including spending the night. My partner caught me at the door before I walked out of there with him. And you know what the weird part was?"

Ms. Bigelow shook her head.

"I'm a pretty smart, retentive person. I know self-defense and I've even won a kickboxing tournament. But this guy interfered with all my defenses. I gave up my control and I didn't even know I was doing it."

The woman nodded, as if all this was resonating. "I remembered something," she said.

Joanna raised her eyebrows, encouraging her to go on.

"He wanted to have sex but I must have told him no. That's why he beat me up. Because I told him no."

Joanna sat back, puzzled. "Good for you for having the guts to say it. But how did you get your volition back? From what I remember from the other night, it seemed so reasonable to do what the guy said, it wouldn't have occurred to me to say no."

Ms. Bigelow lifted a shoulder in a half shrug, and

winced. "Maybe it wears off. Because I remember getting beat up. Definitely remember that."

"Did he say anything? While he was doing it, I mean. Because, you know, beating up a woman who says no is a little extreme. Most guys would drop you at the corner and say better luck next time."

"He said he was entitled." The woman was tiring and her words were losing steam. "To sex. Said it was a— an imperative. That I was supposed to want it."

"Right." What kind of primeval cave had *he* come out of? "I know you're tired, so I only have one more thing."

"Okay." Her eyes closed briefly, then opened when Joanna pulled the picture of Tom Semple out of her handbag.

"Was this the guy?"

Tracey Bigelow looked at the picture for a long time, then shook her head. "No. I think he was older. Maybe five or ten years."

Joanna sat back. It had been a slim chance, but worth taking. "Thank you. You've been an enormous help." She stood. "I'm going, but just between you and me, there's something you should know. And when you get out of here, I want you to pass it on to your girlfriends and coworkers. Anyone who hangs out at the clubs here in town."

The woman nodded, her red hair moving softly on the pillow. *There but for the grace of God—*

Joanna shoved the thought away. "This guy was using some kind of brainwashing technique called the Rules of Seduction. My team is investigating it right now. Tracey, I want you to know that you're in no way responsible for what happened to you. I want you and your friends to be on the watch. Go to a bar or a club, no problem, but go in a group, and don't let anyone leave with someone unless you know him. Can you do that?"

Tracey nodded again.

"We're going to find the ones who are telling these men that it's okay to use violence on a woman to get sex, and we're going to lock them up. I promise you."

Tracey licked her lips. "Thank you. And be careful."

Joanna would have squeezed her hand, but there was an IV line embedded in it. So she had to content herself with an encouraging smile. "Don't worry. I'm on to them now. They won't pull this on me again."

She hoped.

10

Second Rule: It is a man's responsibility and a woman's obligation to fulfill the biological imperative.

Beans & Books
Santa Rita, California
12:20 hours

JOANNA GRABBED A SANDWICH at an espresso bar with a bookstore in the back, and sat in a comfortably upholstered armchair to write up her notes. In this environment of normalcy, with the comfortable chatter of people all around her and the summer sun streaming through the windows onto the shelves of books, the creeped-out feeling began to fade.

Had Thomas Semple gone after the next woman he saw because he'd struck out with Tracey? Weren't they moving fast enough? Was she in some way responsible for what had happened to poor Tracey Bigelow?

No. They were moving as fast as they could, given the information they had. But Tracey's experience told her that these wretched Rules were giving men a sense of entitlement about sex. Teaching them that they deserved what they wanted from women, no matter what the woman's opinion on the subject. If she hadn't been convinced before about how vital it was to shut these people down, she was now.

She made a note recommending that they arrest Thomas Semple, and closed her notebook. After a sip of her coffee and finishing the remainder of her sandwich, she flipped open her cell phone and saw that she had two messages.

She checked the time on the first one. Ten thirty-eight the previous evening? Who could that be?

"I wanted to tell you that I had a good time today." Cooper Maxwell's voice sounded deep and sexy and…agitated. "And that you are an amazing woman. I know we're not going to have much privacy around here, but at some point I want to talk. Alone. We could meet out on the patio. Or somewhere else." A long pause, during which she nearly pressed the button to play the next message. "Well, wish me luck tomorrow. See you in the morning."

Guilt trickled through her. She'd deliberately avoided him last night, deliberately not brought up the subject of what they'd done on the sailboat. She'd laughed and eaten crab and pretended they were both just coworkers on a case and not unexpected lovers who now didn't know how to approach each other.

Because the simple fact was—she didn't know how to handle this. Not once in the years she'd been in law enforcement had she allowed herself to get involved with someone on the job. She'd seen the results of it, and they weren't pretty.

Fair? No. Instructive? Yes.

But I was desperate. I had to know if I was still normal, or if the Rules had messed me up so fundamentally I could no longer trust myself.

And now that she knew they hadn't, what was she going to do about it?

"Nothing" was the obvious answer. But "nothing" didn't seem to work with Cooper Maxwell. He wanted to talk about it. That was a first, in her experience. Usually a guy would take a root canal without anesthetic before he'd come to a woman asking to talk about where the sex went from here.

Well, since they were living in the same house and members of the same team, she couldn't run away. She'd have to find a way to talk to him without Leah and Will around. It had worked before, out on the patio, like he'd suggested. Maybe they could get away with it a second time.

And then she'd have to figure out what to say. Because that was the sixty-four-thousand-dollar question, wasn't it? She couldn't very well tell him the truth—that making love with him had been wild and exciting and she'd do it again in a heartbeat if he wasn't who he was and she wasn't who she was. Talk about mixed messages.

No, the smart thing was to say that it had been wonderful, but it couldn't happen again. They'd have to leave it at that. They had no choice.

Okay, so it wasn't the best decision in the world, but at least it was a decision. Joanna pushed the button to get the next message.

"Hi, it's Leah. Cooper says he wants a conference call with all of us at twelve-thirty to do a status report. Just a heads-up. Later."

Joanna glanced at her watch and drained her coffee. If she hit the gas, she could get back to the safe house in fifteen minutes, and wouldn't need to risk anyone overhearing her report. No matter what the IT guys at CLEU said, anyone who thought a cell phone was secure was deluding himself.

She made it back with enough time to get Leah and Will sandwiches and two minutes to spare. The hot number rang at exactly twelve-thirty. Cooper was taking no chances—evidently he wanted all their situation reports recorded.

"This has been a very enlightening morning," he began. "Have you guys been monitoring the wire?"

"Will and I have," Leah said. "Joanna went to interview an assault victim."

"Another one turned up already?" His tone was sharp.

"The assault happened at three Saturday morning," Joanna said. Succinctly, she outlined what Tracey had told her. "I recommend we pass our information to Santa Rita P.D. Even if there isn't enough evidence to find her attacker or to arrest Thomas Semple, they can still keep an eye on him. And then Leah and I need to track down the earlier victims. I'd be very interested to know if their stories match up."

"I agree," Cooper said. "Have the P.D. interview Semple about any other women he may have been in contact with. See if they can get a list of his fellow classmates, too."

"What about you?" Will asked. "Any luck getting that class list?"

"Not yet, but I'll figure out a way. I tell you, guys, this is the weirdest bunch of crap I've ever heard."

"The problem is, it works," Joanna said soberly.

"And by tomorrow afternoon, I'll know *how* it works," Cooper said. "Stick close to the transmitter, Joanna. I want you to know as much as I know, in real time. This afternoon I plan to bring up whether a woman can resist these Rules. You know, combat them. That'll probably be after the hands-on part of the curriculum."

"I assume that means this Cherise woman. Did you get an ID on her?" Leah wanted to know. "Any chance we can book her on solicitation charges?"

"So far, no," Cooper replied. "All she's done is sit at the front of the class and let herself be turned on. Believe me, I'm watching every move these people make. If we can file charges for anything, I'll find it. Meanwhile, Leah, I want you to do a workup on the instructor. His name is Richard Benton."

Leah scribbled the name on the yellow legal pad in front of her on the console. "I'll have it ready for you when you get back, unless you want me to transmit while you're in class?"

"Yes. I want Joanna and I both to know everything as you and Will dig it up."

"Will do." Leah's pen was poised over her pad. "Anything else?"

"Run this morning's tape by Joanna so she's up to speed. Give me the workup on Richard Benton. Notify P.D. about Thomas Semple. Locate the earlier assault victims." Cooper paused. "That should do it for now. And Joanna?"

"Right here."

"Did you get my voice mail?"

Joanna blinked. Surely he wasn't going to bring that up in front of the others? "Yes."

"I'll want to huddle on that, too, so make some room in your schedule tonight. Okay, team, that's it," he said briskly. "I have half an hour left for lunch break so I'm going to cruise the classroom and hope it's empty. Maybe I'll get lucky and the list will be sitting out on the table."

"Good luck," Will said, and Cooper hung up. Will reached for the wrapped sandwich sitting on the counter. "Looks like we have our work cut out for us."

Leah handed Joanna a set of headphones. "I have the tape from this morning's lesson cued up for you. The counter starts at 09:03 and goes to 12:25. It's three hours of material, but you can skip through some of it, like when the instructor is demonstrating with the model and there are long stretches of silence."

Joanna nodded, and Leah turned back to the computer, where she opened the NCIS database and began a search for information on Richard Benton. Joanna put the headphones on and settled in to learn about the Rules of Seduction. As she listened, she wondered how it was possible that these clueless losers could wind up like Thomas Semple, who had been confident and assured with her, or the other guy who had progressed to violence with Tracey Bigelow. From one end of the emotional scale to the other. Could these classes really do that in two days? And did these Rules affect everyone in the class? Or just a few? Did they affect a man differently if he had a predisposition to violence?

In half an hour she was able to buzz through ninety minutes of tape, skipping the chitchat and silences and focusing intently on the meat of the instruction. By the time Leah signaled her that Cooper was back in session, she had learned enough to understand what Richard Benton was talking about when class resumed and she heard his voice through the transmitter.

"Welcome back. This afternoon we're going to discuss the second of the three Rules. And that is: *It is a man's responsibility and a woman's obligation to fulfill the biological imperative.*"

In the silence, Joanna imagined the members of the class looking at one another, much as she, Will and Leah were doing now.

Cooper said, "Can you explain what you mean by obligation?"

A voice fairly close to him said, "It means the woman has to go along with it. If I want her, she has to want me back. Right?"

"In a way," Benton said. "Remember, the Rules are based on primeval urges that have been, shall we say, paved over by layers and layers of civilization, mores and cultural expectations and restrictions. What we do in these classes is expose the basic biological urges in men and women, and teach you not only how to access them in the deepest parts of the brain, but also how to exploit them. Because in the end, gentlemen, sex is about pleasure as well, isn't it?"

He said he was entitled to sex—Tracey Bigelow's broken whisper echoed in Joanna's memory. *He said it was an imperative.*

What kind of crazy taught men that this was how relationships worked? What kind of sociopath put on classes, soaked the students' brains in antisocial behavior and then went on his merry way, leaving violence and possibly permanent misogyny in his wake?

Joanna swore to herself that, no matter what it took, she was going to shut Richard Benton down.

For the next hour, the three investigators relaxed next to the transmitter and learned about the various ways that a man could break down a woman's resistance and natural caution after the first touches and verbal cues had been successful. Talk about the ick factor. Sick to her stomach, Joanna realized just how Thomas Semple had worked on her, to the point that he'd overlaid her police training and her own self-knowledge with the urge to copulate with him.

At the end of the first break, Cooper spoke quietly into the transmitter.

"Team, I'm out in the hallway with an update. The class list is nowhere to be found. I think Benton has it in his briefcase, if it exists at all. I've seen no sign of it. So I'm going to Plan B. I'm going to circulate a sheet of paper asking for people's info to form a support group. Even if some of these guys don't go wacko and get arrested for assault, maybe I can use it to direct them to therapy. God knows they're going to need it if they ever hope to have normal relationships."

Shortly afterward they heard him propose the plan, and Joanna pictured a wrinkled piece of paper making the rounds of the classroom. Her estimation of Cooper Maxwell's abilities—not to mention his knowledge of how the mind worked—just kept rising. At this rate she was going to have to completely rethink her first opinion of him, which had been colored pretty heavily by her own prejudices and not by reality at all.

She sighed and focused on the tape as the instructor brought Cherise back in.

"Now, with Cherise's permission, I'll demonstrate the complete series of tactile and verbal cues that will change her behavior in keeping with the Second Rule. Before I begin, are there any questions?"

Cooper said, "How can we see this accurately if Cherise is a willing participant? Shouldn't the demonstration be live with a stranger, in some public place?"

The instructor's tone became patient, as if he were speaking to someone who was not very bright. "Yes, of course, that would be an effective way to demonstrate. But the logistics defeat us. You have to admit that taking a class of twenty-three into a club or bar and singling out one woman while providing access for so many to observe would be difficult. We try to keep a low profile, for obvious reasons."

"I suppose," Cooper conceded.

"And there is still the element of resistance to overcome. Cherise, while experienced in our workshops, still has a woman's natural cautions about exposing herself in a public forum. She is not, after all, a sex worker or in the entertainment industry."

The class laughed. When the instructor began, Joanna paid close attention. With every sentence, memory came back. Thomas Semple had said that. And that, too. And when she had done *this,* he had done *this,* which left her following him out of the bar like an obedient puppy. Wow. Semple had had this routine down pat. How many times had he practiced it—and on how many unfortunate women?

She pressed the transmission button on the microphone built into the console. "Cooper, it's Joanna. Whatever Benton is telling Cherise is the exact routine that Thomas Semple went through with me. It's practically word for word. So if we weren't sure before that he'd been in the Rules classes, we can be now."

"Mmm-hmm," Cooper murmured, as if agreeing with some point the instructor had made.

"Joanna out."

"Mmm-hmm."

By the time the instructor had finished explaining what he called the "control switch" and where it was located, Cherise's voice had taken on a dreamy quality. *Great. Another love-bot rolls off the assembly line.* Joanna felt a little sorry for whoever she was dating. How did he counteract all this mumbo jumbo?

"Now it's your turn," Benton said. "Who would like to be the first volunteer?"

"But she's already in a state to obey the imperative," someone objected. "That doesn't give us much of a challenge."

"Ah, but we have more than one workshop assistant," the instructor said over the sound of a door opening. "Gentlemen, meet Andrea."

"Is she single?" a hushed voice close to Cooper wanted to know. "Look at the size of her—"

"She is indeed. Who will be first?"

Don't you dare—

"I will," Cooper said.

Joanna frowned and exchanged a glance with Leah. Cooper was supposed to be gathering information, not placing himself in a position where he could be accused of being involved, if these cases came to trial.

Joanna hit the microphone switch again. "Disengage," she said urgently. "You can't get involved. You're an observer only."

It had nothing to do with his touching Andrea or her big—

"No, *I'm* going first," someone said, and the microphone popped, as if Cooper had been elbowed in the gut.

"All right, all right," he said grudgingly. "Be my guest."

Joanna relaxed in her chair and listened to Bachelor Number Two do his best to find poor Andrea's control switch, which, if she understood correctly, was an energy cluster between the shoulder blades. Unfortunately, the instructor had to prompt him so much that his success seemed limited.

Cooper chuckled, and spoke to someone off to the side. "Look. She's responding to Richard, not to the lawyer guy."

Ick.

Cooper spoke up when it seemed the demonstration was over. "Is there, like, a time limit on the effect of the Rules? In other words, does it wear off, or do the… workshop assistants go home like this?"

"That's a very good question, and thank you for asking," Benton said. "It brings me to the Third Rule, which I wasn't going to get to until tomorrow morning, but consider this a taste of things to come. Yes, the effect has a time limit. An hour, at most. Sometimes only fifteen minutes. Those nasty traditions the body and mind have been subject to throughout a person's upbringing do reassert themselves in a fairly short period. So you need to be prepared for sex, gentlemen, whenever you activate the Rules. Because the Third Rule is: *The biological imperative must be served first, before values, before preferences, even before belief."*

Joanna and Leah turned to one another, and she saw her own dawning realization in Leah's eyes. No wonder some of these men went from shyness to violence so quickly.

The Rules of Seduction were aptly named. These men had been given permission to put themselves above any other kind of rule or law—including those of the state.

Which was precisely where CLEU came in.

11

En route to 144 Vista Mar
Santa Rita, California
18:10 hours

COOPER TUCKED THE sign-up list for the "support group" into his jacket pocket and strode down the hall to the parking lot. Their mission, should he choose to accept it, was to spread through the bars and clubs of Santa Rita this evening to practice what they'd learned in support of the first two Rules. Granted, his classmates probably wouldn't have much in the way of opportunity on a Monday night, but one thing was guaranteed: Joanna would have plenty of suspects to choose from. The only question was how many she could get through in the course of the evening without succumbing to the Rules herself.

He had not had a single chance to find out how the Rules could be counteracted. During the Q and A period this afternoon, Richard Benton had fielded a flood of "what-if" scenarios and spent most of the forty-five minutes calming fears and going over meridian points in hopes of reassuring his horny but jittery students. And then he'd packed up his briefcase and bolted before Cooper could even open his mouth.

Good thing he still had tomorrow. He'd find out what he needed to know and then he'd arrange for the locals to put a surveillance on Benton. If the guy was going to set up shop in another town, Cooper wanted to be the first to know about it.

That is, if they didn't find a reason to nail him here in Santa Rita first.

He pulled into the driveway at the safe house and found Joanna, Will and Leah in the comm room. Joanna, headphones on, didn't turn around until she saw Leah get up to hand him the material on Richard Benton. Then she slipped the headphones off and gave him a professional smile.

He didn't know what he'd been hoping for, but he supposed that was as much as he could expect. And they both knew that he wanted to talk to her sometime tonight. He didn't know when, but he would make sure it happened.

"You survived the first day," she said by way of greeting.

"I should be getting hazard pay." He flipped through the printout on Benton. "This class is an assault on any thinking man's brain."

"I don't think the upstairs brain is the part they're going for," Leah observed. "Do these guys seriously buy into this biological imperative crap?"

Cooper looked up. "You heard what a free-for-all the Q and A period was. Every single guy was convinced that Benton held the answer to his personal problem."

"And that answer is to take what he wants, regardless of what the woman says." Will sounded as though he still couldn't believe it. "Like you say, these guys are going to need major therapy."

"I hope that's all they need. But now we know the motivation behind many of these assaults. They all figure they're entitled to sex, and when the woman refuses, they force her." Cooper glanced at Joanna. "Which means we have to be even more careful tonight."

That prickly pride he'd seen at Kellan's wedding straightened Joanna's spine, and she laid the headphones carefully on the console. "Obviously, I've come to that conclusion myself. Even if all of them don't give in to the permission to be violent, a few of them might. Too bad you weren't able to find out what the evasive moves are."

He would not rise to the bait. If she was trying to pick a fight in order to stave off their little talk, she was going to fail.

"I'll make sure I ask the questions tomorrow. We're going to be in place at least until the weekend, when I'm expecting a lot of activity. In the meantime, your best bet is to not let anyone touch you."

"That could get interesting," Leah said. "The guy's whole goal is to touch her and interrupt her meridian flow or whatever."

"True." Cooper glanced at Joanna. "You'll have to keep a table between you and the suspect at all times. Keep your back to a wall so his partner—we're supposed to be operating in pairs, remember—can't come to his rescue."

"Or you could follow Joanna from place to place and make sure you're the one hitting on her," Will suggested.

Joanna shook her head. "That negates the point. What I'm trying to do here is resist, right? So that the longer the guy tries, the more frustrated he gets, and the greater the chances this 'imperative' brainwashing might kick in. When he tries to assault me, I whip out the cuffs, you guys come out of the woodwork and off he goes to lockup." She paused and looked at Cooper. "Or am I missing something?"

Cooper had to smile. "Since we haven't actually discussed the stakeout scenario, I'd say you haven't missed anything at all." He turned to the others. "Joanna's right. Tonight is an experiment. If what she's outlined actually happens, it will confirm what we suspect about why these waves of violence follow these workshops." He glanced at her, then back to the others. "Joanna brings up a good point. Not everyone is going to respond to the Rules by getting violent. Maybe only a few do."

"But which few, is the question," Will put in.

"People who have been violent before," Leah said suddenly. "Maybe some of your classmates have records. I could find out."

"Good thinking," Cooper said to her. "But for tonight, we're going to limit Joanna's contact with them to only one, for two reasons. A, we don't want to tip off Richard Benton and the people in the class that law enforcement is on to them. And B, we don't want the danger to Joanna to escalate."

"I'm all for that," Joanna said. "From what I can tell from the wire, there are going to be at least three pairs of guys in each place tonight, so the odds are stacked against me from the start." She glanced at Cooper. "And there's no guarantee you'll be in the same places I am, is there?"

There was no way he'd let anyone drag him out of any club Joanna was in, and not just because he was her team leader, either. "I'll guarantee it," he said quietly. "I'm supposed to team up with a lawyer called Julian Royden. We're meeting at Club Koko at nine, so, Will, you'll be in position by eight forty-five, and, Joanna, that'll be your starting point. I'll direct Royden's attention to you, and we'll start with him. At least that way you'll know nobody will be sneaking up on you."

She nodded. "Good plan. Thanks."

The pride had faded from her gaze and in it he saw only quiet professionalism and something else that was hard to define. A sense that she felt safe, maybe? Not that these weren't qualities he wanted to see in all of his team members, but it seemed to mean more when he saw it in Joanna.

She felt safe with him. She felt wild and exciting pleasure with him, too, he knew that. Those were good starting points, weren't they?

Starting points for what? What are you thinking? Are you nuts?

No, of course not. He only knew that he was going to keep Joanna safe tonight…even if it meant seducing her himself.

THE CITY PARKING lot behind Club Koko backed up against a wood fence. Cooper eased their unmarked vehicle into the last open space and turned the engine off.

"Leah, we're parked behind Koko. Let us know when Will gets set up inside, and when he spots Royden."

Leah acknowledged the orders, and Joanna reached under her silky top to toggle off the little microphone taped to her middle. It wasn't strictly necessary to turn off her transmitter, of course, but he'd just as soon prefer that whatever they said in this vehicle while they waited would not be recorded for everyone in the department to hear.

These few minutes were a gift, and after waiting all this time for a chance to get her alone, he planned to take advantage of them.

Or maybe he'd gotten ahead of himself. The silence between them was broken only by muffled conversations as people strolled by on the sidewalk twenty feet away. In the dark, the fence behind them made it hard for anyone to see their silhouettes in the car, and other vehicles hemmed them in on both sides. It was the perfect setup in which to wait. And talk.

As soon as he figured out the best way to bring up the subject on his mind.

"Any particular reason we're maintaining radio silence?" Joanna asked quietly.

"I think you know."

"If it has anything to do with the voice mail you left me earlier, I don't think this is the time or the place. Will is going to signal us any minute. And I need to keep my head in this game, not be distracted by…personal things."

"That may be true, but when will it be the time and the place? Tomorrow, when I'm in class? Next week? When we close the case?"

"Door number three sounds good."

"It's hard to open door number three when you'll have been posted back to L.A. and I'll be in San Francisco."

"I rest my case."

What was it about this woman that she didn't want to talk? Granted, he wasn't the chattiest guy in the world when it came to matters of the heart, but they were adults. They should be able to discuss this in a rational fashion. Talk about role reversal.

"What is your case, Joanna? Because I'd like to know where I stand, just in case you've tried and convicted me already and forgot to tell me."

She shook her head. "That's a little dramatic. But even you have to admit this is starting to interfere with our ability to work together. I mean, we're supposed to be focused on our jobs, on keeping our stories straight, not grabbing the few minutes we have to bring up subjects that can't go anywhere."

His silence acknowledged that she was right.

"We can't do this while we're on this op together, and that's that."

But it didn't seem to change anything—including the fact that he could smell the scent of her skin and hair each time she moved, or that the light from the street lamp behind the fence was glinting on the liquid curves of the silk that covered her breasts.

No, it didn't change the facts, and the fact was, he wanted her. Here in the car, back at the safe house, in some hotel room that he had no doubt Julian Royden had all ready to go.

"What are you afraid of?" he asked softly.

Wrong thing to say. Her spine straightened and the soft curves of lip and cheek turned hard with offense.

"Oh, I get it. I'm not stopping this because it's policy or because it's the right thing to do. I'm stopping it because I'm afraid. Then you get to feel superior. Well, enjoy it, for what it's worth. I don't care."

Just what lay at the root of that kind of bitterness? What had she been through in her past relationships that had taught her this? "You know that wasn't what I meant."

"How do you know what I think?"

"I don't. I'm trying to find out." There was nothing to do but take the plunge into brutal honesty. He may never have another chance, and he was for sure not going to let her walk away thinking…what she was thinking. "All I know is that what happened on the boat was great, and I don't just mean making love. I thought that we put aside what we are in uniform and came together like we were real. Just two people crazy for each other."

She said nothing. The light of the street lamp outlined her nose and cheek in silver, leaving her eyes in darkness.

"I want to get to know that woman better," he finished quietly. "That's all I wanted to say, even if it's taken me twenty-four hours to get there."

She didn't move, except to nibble her lip, as though she were making up her mind to something. In the silence, he heard her take a quick breath. "There's something you should know about—"

"Cooper. Joanna," Leah said in both their ears. "It's show time. Will says there's a table for three at the window, and a man whose description matches Royden's driver's license photo is sitting there facing the door. Will is at the bar about ten feet away."

Cooper glanced at Joanna, then reached under his shirt and turned his transmitter on. She did the same. "Copy that. We're on our way."

They'd only had a few minutes, he reflected as Joanna walked into the club and ordered something to drink. From the door, he caught Royden's eye and nodded toward her. But in those minutes at least he'd been able to say what he needed to.

The next move was up to her.

12

WHAT JOANNA LIKED best about silk was how sexy it made her feel. She liked the smooth, cool slide of it on her skin and the way it clung to her curves, suggesting more than revealing. If it hadn't been for the conversation in the car, she could have walked in here like she owned the place, and it wouldn't have been an act. But as things stood, she had to put on the best performance she knew how for the sake of the job.

What she really wanted to do was run away and hide. And then call Carleen for some moral support.

She'd chosen this burnt-orange cami trimmed with skinny black-velvet ribbon to get attention, and now she had to go through with it. She'd intercepted a few glances as she'd sipped her glass of wine, waiting for Cooper to exchange pleasantries with their target and then approach her. So at least that part was working. Now she just had to wrestle her focus off the personal and onto the professional.

Using her peripheral vision, she studied their target.

Leah had already run the workup on him. A J.D. from Stanford Law School, Julian Royden owned one vehicle—a hybrid, what else—and had a record so clean it squeaked, except for a couple of juvenile offenses whose details had been closed. Had they been violent? Or were they just misdemeanors like petty theft? She'd give a lot to know.

When Joanna saw him tip his head back and laugh at something Cooper had said, she had to remind herself that these were supposed to be two complete strangers she knew nothing about. She needed to be careful that nothing showed on her face but polite interest when they approached her.

Which they did, a couple of minutes later, after another glass of wine appeared at her elbow with their compliments.

"Gentlemen, that was kind of you," she said with a welcoming smile as she walked over to their table. "I hope this means I can join you."

Cooper got up and pulled out the chair opposite him, while Julian sat on her left, facing the window. They introduced themselves while Joanna amused herself making up an on-the-spot persona. Luckily, Carleen wasn't here to realize it was *her* persona—but at least Joanna wouldn't trip herself up while she was giving the facts of a life she knew as well as her own.

The first rule of successful undercover work was to make up as little as you needed to. The bad guys might be stupid, but they did pay attention.

Cooper had barely had a chance to ask her how she liked nursing when Julian made his move. As she reached for her wine with her left hand, he slid a palm

The Harlequin Reader Service® — Here's how it works:

Accepting your 2 free books and 2 free gifts places you under no obligation to buy anything. You may keep the books and gifts and return the shipping statement marked "cancel." If you do not cancel, about a month later we'll send you 4 additional books and bill you just $3.99 each in the U.S. or $4.47 in Canada, plus 25¢ shipping & handling per book and applicable taxes if any.* That's the complete price and — compared to cover prices of $4.75 each in the U.S. and $5.75 each in Canada — it's quite a bargain! You may cancel at any time, but if you choose to continue, every month we'll send you 4 more books, which you may either purchase at the discount price or return to us and cancel your subscription.

*Terms and prices subject to change without notice. Sales tax applicable in N.Y. Canadian residents will be charged applicable provincial taxes and GST. All orders subject to approval. Credit or debit balances in a customer's account(s) may be offset by any other outstanding balance owed by or to the customer. Please allow 4 to 6 weeks for delivery.

If offer card is missing write to: The Harlequin Reader Service, 3010 Walden Ave., P.O. Box 1867, Buffalo, NY 14240-1867

NO POSTAGE
NECESSARY
IF MAILED
IN THE
UNITED STATES

BUSINESS REPLY MAIL

FIRST-CLASS MAIL   PERMIT NO. 717-003   BUFFALO, NY

POSTAGE WILL BE PAID BY ADDRESSEE

HARLEQUIN READER SERVICE
3010 WALDEN AVE
PO BOX 1867
BUFFALO NY 14240-9952

under hers and she felt him trying to find the meridian point on her wrist. He might have had better luck if he hadn't been so fascinated with her cleavage.

"Julian," she teased, pulling her hand away, "no holding hands until we know each other a little better."

He flushed, and she felt kind of bad that she had to be the one to make him fail. He'd probably make some girl a nice, faithful boyfriend if he'd just wake up and see his own value instead of depending on these crackpot theories that, unfortunately, only got him what he thought he wanted.

Cooper leaned back in his chair and toyed with his beer glass. "You could pretend you know him." His smile was open and friendly, but his eyes held a message.

Pretend.

"I guess I could, at that." She smiled at Julian. "Any man who buys me a glass of wine is a friend of mine."

She reached over and squeezed his hand, allowing his fingertips to tickle her wrist. She wasn't a hundred percent sure where the mystery meridian was, but she'd bet he wasn't, either.

A glance at Cooper told her she'd interpreted his message correctly. It told her something else, too. His gaze was steady, but the depths of his eyes held the knowledge that they had unfinished business together. The question was, did he just want to talk some more, or did he plan on a reprise of that amazing hour on the boat?

At the thought, her nipples tightened.

Julian sat up straight, and glanced at Cooper as though looking for his acknowledgment that he'd scored. Cooper nodded and said, "You two get acquainted. I'll be back."

One table over, Will toyed with a glass of iced tea and gave Joanna a reassuring look over Julian's shoulder. She knew Cooper had to make himself scarce so that he couldn't be connected to the police. But still, he left a void in her confidence that not even Will could fill. She took a deep breath, turned back to Julian and went into full love-bot mode. With Thomas Semple, the entire process had taken only a few minutes. She had Julian out of the bar and onto the street in less, with Will a careful distance behind.

"Where are we going?" she asked dreamily, clinging to Julian's arm. It prevented him from slipping it around her shoulders and going for that tendon, but he didn't need to know that.

The Rules were having quite an effect on Julian. His shoulders were straight, his chest puffed out in triumph and his step was firm as they walked up the street. What a difference between this man and the uncertain lawyer in the horn-rimmed glasses she'd first seen at the table with Cooper. Again, she wished that a woman's love could do this for him instead of the Rules.

"I have a room at the Pacific Hotel, up here at the end of the block."

"A room?" Whoa. None of the previous assaults had taken place in a hotel room. Two parking garages, an alley and the back hallway of a club, yes, but not a hotel room. How were Will and Cooper going to cover her there? Setting up a surveillance post in an adjoining hotel room could be done on short notice, but not on no notice at all.

"Joanna," Leah said in the transmitter in her ear, "Cooper says to abort. No go on the hotel room."

How could she abort when chances were good that at least four of Cooper's classmates had seen her leave with Julian? If she went back to Club Koko to try with someone else, it would be obvious the Rules hadn't worked the first time, and someone might try a little harder. She'd be in greater danger of losing control of the situation. Not only that, she'd bet ten bucks that a disappointed Julian would follow her back there and maybe cause a scene.

No, it was best to skip the center line and go straight for the offensive zone.

"I got a king-size bed," Julian confided. "I figured we'd use all the space."

Joanna slowed her pace. "I don't want to go to a hotel."

"Why not?"

Lucky thing she was good at thinking on her feet. "They're dirty. You can get diseases just by walking across the carpet."

He patted the hand that lay on his arm, and felt up her wrist, as though he was making sure she was still under the influence of the Rules. "Not at the Pacific, honey. It's a four-star place."

They were nearly at the hotel now. She needed to bring this to a head, fast.

"Can't we go to your house?" she whined.

"I live miles away from here. That's why I booked the room, see?"

"Where?"

"At the Pacific." Man, does this stuff affect brain activity, too?

"I know that. I mean, where do you live?"

"In San Jose. But that doesn't matter. Here we are."

"No." She pulled her hand away from his arm and stepped back. "I don't want to."

"Of course you do. Come on. I'm real anxious to get to know you better."

Joanna turned and took a few steps back in the direction they'd come, passing Will, who gave her a quizzical look before he stopped to look at something in a shop window.

She felt a heavy hand on her shoulder. *Uh-oh. No sensitive tendon for you, buddy.* She'd just spotted the access alley for the hotel's domestic deliveries. If a guy was going to attempt an assault, that'd be the place to do it.

A quick bend and twist, and she was out from under those probing fingers. Two more steps and she'd be at the alley's mouth.

"Look, honey, be a clean freak if you want, but you're still coming with me."

"Why?" she prodded, backing into the alley. "Why do I have to?"

"Because you want to." Over his shoulder, she saw Will come into view. "Deep inside you want me to have you, and I'm going to."

"How do you know?"

"It's a biological imperative."

"A what?"

"I'll explain later. I'm getting tired of this." He grabbed her wrist.

Gotcha! Joanna stomped on his instep and shoved him in the gut. Julian never saw it coming, nor did he see the double-elbow jab to the nape of his neck that laid him out on the concrete.

While he recovered, Joanna whipped her cuffs out of her handbag and snapped them on, then hauled him to his feet. "Julian Royden, you're under arrest for assaulting a police officer. Will," she said over her shoulder, "I trust the P.D. is on its way?"

"Right here." Will stepped aside and two uniformed cops gripped Julian's upper arms and walked him away. The last glimpse she had of him was a dazed look of utter confusion as his brain tried to compute what had just happened.

Okay, so maybe the elbow jab hadn't been strictly necessary. But perhaps Tracey Bigelow would agree that it evened up the score a little.

She rolled her shoulders and touched the place where Julian had grabbed her. She might even have a bruise in the morning.

"You okay?" Cooper materialized at the mouth of the alley and she and Will joined him.

"Yes," she said. "Who's next?"

"Nobody's next," Cooper replied. "You're off duty."

She stared at him. "Why? It's early yet. I'll interview Royden down at the P.D. and then I'll come back."

"You just beat the crap out of a lawyer. Aren't you going to call it a night?"

"One jab does not constitute a beating—"

"It would if it had been him dishing it out."

"And besides, he grabbed me. Will saw it. Ask him."

But Will had very diplomatically paused a short distance away to gaze into another shop window. Joanna snorted. *Coward.*

"Joanna, I'm well aware that you need anger management training, but on top of that, you disobeyed a direct order to abort the bait."

"I do not need anger management training," she said hotly. "I wasn't angry at all. The guy made a move on me. I defended myself. What did you want me to do, let him knock out a few teeth so you'd feel justified?"

"That was a low blow," he gritted. "And it doesn't distract me. Why did you ignore my order?"

She leaned into his face. If she hadn't been angry before, she sure as heck was now. "Because it was a stupid order. Our mission was to get him to try to assault me. That happened. What are you complaining about?"

"I am not complaining," he enunciated. "I'm showing concern for a teammate in physical danger."

"I was never in danger," she scoffed. "Did you see me—"

"Dammit, Joanna!" With a glance over his shoulder at Will, who was hanging back well out of earshot, Cooper muscled her into the nearest doorway.

And then his mouth came down on hers.

Oh, my God.

Desire rocketed up between them as Joanna wrapped her arms around his neck and met his force with her own. Her lips parted and his tongue took hers with masterful intent, sliding its length, probing the depths of her mouth with such heat that a flash bomb of her own detonated deep in her belly.

He broke the kiss and put both hands on her waist, setting her away from him with a gesture of finality.

"For the last time," he said hoarsely, "I aborted the

bait because I thought you were in danger and we couldn't cover you. Please don't take the investigation into your own hands and force us to operate on the fly. That's how investigators get killed."

Her mouth dropped open a little as she realized just how deep the concern in his eyes went. And it was more than concern. He really cared about what happened to her. And regardless of how well-equipped she was to take care of herself, that concern was what motivated him, not any male sense of superiority.

This was not the men in her L.A. subdivision. This was Cooper Maxwell. Not a commander talking to his troops, but a man talking to the woman he'd made love to only yesterday—a man afraid for his woman's safety.

The breath backed up in her lungs and she spoke with difficulty. "I—I'm sorry. Honestly. It won't happen again."

He relaxed, and gave her a smile that melted her all the way down to her toes. "Thanks. Sorry I had to be a hardnose."

"I meant about disobeying a direct order. After I get back, I still think we should try for another one of your classmates."

Nine men out of ten would have blown up all over again and sent her into a permanent state of frustrated resentment. But Cooper was in that small percentage of men who seemed to listen when a woman spoke.

"Why's that?" He glanced over his shoulder and gave Will the all-clear sign. Joanna had to smile as the younger man ambled up cautiously.

"You and I may be recognized, so we're out of commission for this round, but Will isn't," she said. "I vote we shadow him in the vehicle. He can tail a couple leaving the bar on foot. You never know. Maybe we can save another woman tonight."

Cooper gave her a considering look, then glanced at Will. "Are you up for that?"

He nodded, obviously trying to lay a cool veneer over his eagerness. "Yessir."

"Great," Joanna said. "So when I come back from interviewing Royden, I'll—"

"You said it yourself, Joanna," Cooper interrupted. "You're out of commission tonight. After you finish the interview, you'll go to the safe house. Will and I can do this surveillance alone. No bait."

"But—" She stopped herself as she caught a glimpse of Will's face. The eagerness had been replaced with confusion as she argued with their team leader. *For once in your life, Joanna, can you do what's right instead of trying to justify yourself?* It was one thing to disobey an order. It was another to undermine Cooper's authority in front of everyone, including Leah, who was still monitoring their communications.

She'd said it herself a few seconds ago. She'd promised not to flout him, hadn't she?

Yes, it grated on her. But what had Bella told her once? Sometimes you just had to take one for the team.

"Right," she said. "I'll do the interview and meet you back at the house. Good luck."

Cooper nodded and their gazes connected as he handed her the keys to his vehicle. Then he turned to follow Will back to his car.

She'd seen a lot of emotions in his eyes since they'd met on the weekend. Desire, fear, even anger. But now there was something new—something she'd hungered for without knowing she needed it.

She'd seen respect.

13

Downtown
Santa Rita, California
00:17 hours

COOPER STARTED WILL'S CAR and pulled out of the lot, driving at a normal pace past Will and the couple he was tailing, up to the end of the block.

"Leah, I recognize the male from class. His name is Darren Phillips. Two *L*s. Run a workup on him and let us know, then find out if Will knows where they're going," he said.

In a few moments, the reply came back. "Darren Phillips, aged thirty-two, employed as a software engineer. Drives a 2004 Lexus. No record, no warrants. Not even a parking ticket." She paused, then came back on. "Will says Phillips mentioned a walk in the park."

Perfect. "Alert the P.D., would you, to stand by in case we need an arrest." Cooper kept going, turned left and parked on the street that bordered the rose garden and the bit of woods that made up the city park.

He got out and lost himself in the shadows under the trees. In a few moments the couple passed him, talking quietly. The woman even laughed at something Darren said. Pretty harmless. If Joanna was right and the Rules triggered violence only in people who had those tendencies already, maybe this woman would be okay.

They'd find out shortly.

Again his thoughts wandered to Joanna. He hoped that nothing would get messed up down at the P.D. during the booking process. Julian would be charged and released pending his court date, but not until the workshop was over. At least, that was the plan. All he needed was for Julian to show up tomorrow and announce Cooper's identity to the whole class. Between Julian and Thomas Semple, you'd think they would have enough evidence to charge Richard Benton, but the law didn't work that way. Somehow they had to get something on him.

"Santa Rita P.D. is standing by," Leah said in Cooper's ear transmitter.

The couple emerged on the other side of the park and climbed the steps of a house on the corner. Cooper tensed as Darren leaned in for a kiss on the woman's cheek. Then the man straightened, pulled a card from his wallet and handed it to her. As she went inside, Darren loped down the steps and back through the park, his stride jaunty, as though walking a woman to her door was a huge accomplishment.

Maybe it was.

"Leah, ask the P.D. to stand down. It looks like Joanna was right and the Rules don't affect everyone. Luckily for that woman."

"Acknowledged. Will wants to know what the plan is now."

"Ask him to join me."

Will had barely settled himself into the passenger seat when their transmitters clicked.

"Cooper," Leah's voice said, "I'm going to switch all three of your transmitters to the active channel so all of you can receive as well as send. Joanna is down at the station interviewing the suspect, and there's a very interesting conversation going on."

A couple of clicks, and he heard Joanna's voice clearly. "I don't care who you are. As far as I'm concerned, you're a sorry-ass excuse of a man using these damn Rules of Seduction to get laid. Now sit down and don't move."

Cooper sighed and ran a hand through his hair. Had Joanna never heard of Good Cop? Did she only play Bad Cop?

"How did you know about that?" the lawyer's voice rose with every word. "That's supposed to be confidential."

"Right. How to rape a woman in ten easy lessons. And cheer up. Maybe you'll get a closed courtroom for your trial."

"Listen. I want to cut a deal."

Cooper could practically see Joanna roll her eyes. "Right, like you were willing to cut me a deal, right before you attacked me? Tell it to the D.A."

"No, I'm serious." The lawyer's voice became edged with panic. "We have to keep this quiet. I could lose all my clients."

"My heart bleeds."

In spite of himself, Cooper grinned. Joanna had obviously figured out the right approach to use with

Royden. She could teach newbie investigators a thing or two about balls.

"But one of my clients is Afrodita Enterprises!"

He straightened in the driver's seat. "Joanna, that's one of the dummy corporations the workshops do business under," he said urgently. "Play along with him. See what we can get."

"I'm listening," Joanna told the lawyer. "Officer, may I see his ID?" A brief pause, then, "All right, Julian Royden, why don't you start with telling me why you're taking these lame workshops?"

"I would think that would be obvious," Royden said with some bitterness. "I have trouble with relationships. I needed help."

"You're right there," Joanna said, and in the darkened car, Will smothered a chuckle.

"Obviously it's a bunch of crap," Royden said. "It doesn't work. I feel personally injured and misled, and I regret any harm I may have done to you."

"I'm sure you do. Let's get to the point, Mr. Royden. Tell me about Afrodita Enterprises."

"Right. Well, they're a California corporation based in Monterey, where the payments from the students are processed. They retained me a year ago to draw up the incorporation papers and file for their licenses with the state."

"And?"

"And so, in exchange for keeping this quiet and letting me go, I'll give you information about the executive board."

"So you're aware that there's something fishy about their line of business. Otherwise, why give up a legitimate enterprise?"

"Oh, their incorporation is aboveboard," Julian said. "My work is sound. But obviously what they're teaching is bogus."

"It's not bogus, Mr. Royden. I've been a victim of the Rules myself, so I know that for a fact. But they're telling you and your fellow students that you're entitled to sex no matter what, and that is very dangerous to the female victims."

"The Rules worked on you?" Royden sounded puzzled. "I must be doing something wrong, then."

Cooper figured the guy had just come within inches of being slapped upside the head, because it took a moment for Joanna to speak again, and when she did, she bit the words off one by one.

"Regardless. I want the guys who are running this show."

"There's the instructor, Richard Benton," Julian said eagerly.

"Yeah, yeah, I know about him already. Is he one of the players behind this?"

"He's a member of the board."

"Does he use the Rules himself?"

"I don't know. I don't see why he wouldn't. He's good at it."

"Okay, who else?"

"Agree to a deal first."

"Mr. Royden, you are in no position to make demands."

"I think I am. You need information, and I have it."

"Give me what you've got and I'll tell you what I can do."

"No. I need assurance."

"All right," Joanna conceded. "We'll drop the attempted rape charge and proceed in good faith, depending on the accuracy of your information."

"Good. Fine. Okay, I'll tell you the names of the operating board members."

"I already know that. Most of them are fakes."

"But not all of them."

"I'm not even going to bring up what happens to people who falsify information on legal documents," Joanna said. "What do you mean, not all of them?"

"Three of the names are fakes. But Richard Benton isn't. And the fifth name is fake, but he's a real person. Tony Bingham."

"Who? Who's that last one?"

"He's based in L.A. Kind of a shady character. I've heard he has mob connections, but that's probably just PR."

"Anthony 'Bling' Bingham?" Joanna's tone sharpened. "Dark hair, brown eyes, in his early thirties?"

"No. That would be the kid. He's small potatoes compared to his dad, from what I hear."

"You've got that right," Joanna said grimly. "Thank you, Mr. Royden. You've been very helpful."

"What do you know about this Tony Bingham?"

Cooper pulled away from the Santa Rita P.D. building and Joanna relaxed for the first time that night. The interior of the car felt like a haven of safety compared to what she'd seen tonight.

She wasn't quite sure what had prompted Will and Cooper to join her in the city P.D.'s parking lot after her interview with Royden, but she was feeling so drained that she'd been only too happy to hand the keys to Cooper and let him take her back to the safe house.

"Not a lot," she admitted. "But I bet he knows me, since I put his boy in the hospital for trying to turn my best friend's baby sister into a hooker."

Cooper slanted her a glance and said nothing. His hands controlled the wheel, sure and strong, the way they controlled the sensations in a woman's body—

Stop that.

Obviously, she needed some sleep. Or a good dose of self-control. Or a plane ticket to anywhere as long as it was out of reach of the scent of his cologne.

She blew a resigned breath up through her bangs and tried to focus. "Okay, so it's time to come clean. That's why I was assigned this case. Bella said that if I helped your unit get these jokers off the streets, my commander would expunge the violence from my record."

"Right. The punishment detail."

She made a rueful face. "Don't cast that up to me. I don't think that anymore. I do police work so I can make a difference, and I'm really seeing that in this case. What I've worked for all of my career is right here."

In the silence, she heard her own words, and wondered if he'd picked up on the Freudian slip. Other things she'd wanted for a long time were right here, too. As in, sitting there in the driver's seat.

How many lead investigators would have let her run this evening's operation? Granted, Cooper had to stay out of sight so his classmates wouldn't identify him, but he could have been micromanaging every single moment of it through Leah and the transmission network. Instead, he'd let Joanna do what she did best— operate on the fly, responding to the situation as it changed so they could prevent what could have been a disaster. She'd done the interview when technically it had been his job. He'd stood back and let her negotiate the deal with Julian Royden without even a cautionary lecture. And he'd made it obvious to the guys at the P.D. who were their safety net that she was as much to be reckoned with as he was, to the point that one of them had even thought she was running the case.

In short, Cooper was not the arrogant groper she'd assumed he was. He was strong enough to let her do what had to be done, while running the operation with respect for every person on the team.

And he was a terrific kisser.

And made love like a dream.

No, she wasn't going to think about that. She'd laid down the ground rules and she could not be the one to break them.

"If I asked Leah to do a workup on Tony Bingham, any idea what she'd find?" Cooper broke the silence by getting back to business, for which Joanna was grateful. She needed to rein in her runaway thoughts before they got her into trouble. Again.

"We know he has gang connections, not the mob, as our lawyer friend said," she replied slowly. "His son, Bling, is a small-time heroin dealer when he's not forcing working girls into his stable. I'm betting he gets his product from his dad, but I've never been able to pin anything on Tony. The guy has his fingers in any number of pies, as long as they're stuffed with money."

"Which Afrodita Enterprises seems to be."

"The legitimate face of it must have appealed to him. From all accounts, he does have a real chain of dry-cleaning businesses. He could be straight but he chooses not to be. That would be too much work, I guess."

Cooper spun the wheel and pulled into the driveway at the safe house. Will's truck sat out front, and all the windows were dark except for those in the comm room. Maybe Leah was still up, though their transmitters were off and work was officially done for the night. That would be good. Being alone with Cooper under any cir-cumstances was a bad idea right now.

The garage door slid up and Cooper parked the unmarked police vehicle inside and shut off the engine. When he made no move to get out, Joanna looked at him curiously. The dim glow from the automatic overhead light lit his cheekbones and gave his face a starkness it didn't possess in daylight.

"Earlier, you said you had something to tell me," he said.

"Oh." *Get out of here, quick.* She fumbled with the seat belt and released it. "Never mind. Forget it."

"Was it work-related?"

"Um, no." Good grief, where was the door release? Window, lock, seat control…too many stupid buttons in these cars.

"Joanna."

"What? Where is the door handle?"

"I want you to tell me before we go in. Whatever you have on your mind."

No way was she going to tell him that the only reason she'd made love with him on that boat was so that she could reassure herself her responses were normal. No way was she going to admit she'd used him. He'd been terrific, and she'd been manipulative. He'd been sincere, and she'd been hiding her motives...even from herself.

"It was nothing. All resolved." Ah, *there* it was.

Click!

The automatic locks slid down, and the handle lifted fruitlessly under her fingers. "Hey!"

"Just for a minute," Cooper said. "I want to talk about what we don't have resolved."

Joanna didn't waste time pretending she didn't know what he meant. She needed to get out of this car before she lost all her carefully constructed reasons why she shouldn't crawl into his lap and kiss him until he begged for mercy.

"I have it resolved," she said.

"Do you? Then how come you're looking at me like that?"

Busted.

He'd made his point, so he flipped the locks open again. "Look, Joanna, I heard what you said about nothing happening between us while we're working together. I know that in my head, but meantime my body is going crazy being this close to you and not being able to touch you."

Ohhhh, help. If ever there was a way to melt a woman's heart, this was it. She had to do something, quick.

This time her fingers went straight to the door handle and she pushed it open. She'd just made it to the back of the car, with the door to the garage in arm's reach, when he caught her.

"I didn't peg you for the running-away type."

"I'm not."

"It's just me, huh?" Hand over hand up her arm, he reeled her in, closer and closer.

"No, it's not you, it's me," she blurted. "Don't you see? You drive me just as crazy but we can't. Get it? We can't!"

And I can't do this with my stupid lie between us. I'm not as honorable as you. I like you more than is good for me, but I let you make love to me so I could use you.

"We're off duty." He pulled her against him and every cell in her body yearned toward him. How was a woman supposed to fight this? Regulations and principles were doomed when they went up against the sheer force of desire.

She opened her lips to say something—what, she didn't know—and then it was too late for words. His mouth captured hers, telling her, *We're not arguing about this another second,* in the most primal terms. And she answered the same way, her lips softening and angling across his, opening and surrendering until she lost herself completely in his kiss. He pulled her closer, moving his feet apart so that he could fit his hips against the soft welcome of hers—

Oh, yes—

And so she could feel the hard demand of his erection riding against her.

At that, she lost her grip on her control. Yes, Leah was probably wondering why it was taking so long to park the car. Yes, they were breaking regulations. Yes, she had protested.

But none of it seemed to matter when his mouth was so hot and his body so hard and his shoulders felt so damn good under her hands, especially when she slipped them under the collar of his shirt and felt the heat of his naked skin in the dark.

Sometime in the last minute, the overhead light had gone out, as though something out there was giving them both permission and privacy.

Her universe lost its reference points. There was only the dark and the heat and Cooper and she was drowning in all three. He ran his hands up her rib cage, under the silk of her burnt-orange camisole.

"Tell me you're not wearing a bra under this," he whispered, then nibbled her earlobe.

"Sorry to disappoint you." She grinned and nibbled back, taking a moment to use the tip of her tongue to discover several sensitive places on his earlobe and the side of his neck.

He cupped her breasts through her bra and moved back so that he could kiss his way along her jawline and down her throat to the exposed curves. How was it possible for a person to lose the rest of the world so completely? Because all her world could contain was the way his mouth felt on her breasts, hot and damp and oh, so skilled. The straps of both bra and camisole fell down along her arms. There was something terribly naughty and yet restrained about not being stripped—because he only made love to what he could reach without undressing her.

Her cleavage was loving it.

He pulled down her neckline and hooked her bra's cup with one finger, just enough to expose her nipple. "Mmm," he murmured, licking it. "I like it when you're so turned on your nipples are as hard as my cock."

"Suck me," she begged. "I love your mouth on me."

She groaned as he obliged her, swirling his tongue over her aching nipple, taking it in his mouth and nibbling as he suckled.

With a sudden movement, he lifted her up onto the trunk of the car. "That's better." He released her other nipple from its prison and settled back to his pleasurable task. "Now you're right where I want you."

"Oh, just pull this off," she begged, struggling against the fragile confinement of her camisole.

"No." His tongue swirled over her smooth cleavage. "What if someone comes out to see why we're taking so long?"

"They won't."

"I kinda like seeing how turned on you can get with all your clothes on. Want me to make your nipples hard when we debrief, just by looking at you?"

"Brat," she panted.

"I could lick you in the car," he whispered, demonstrating with his swirling tongue. "Walk up behind you in the interview room and slip my hands under your blouse to fondle your beautiful breasts. Like this. No one would know."

His big hands felt wonderful on her flesh. "There are c-cameras in the interview rooms."

"Then we'd be turning on more than just ourselves, wouldn't we?" he suggested wickedly against her curves. "Those guys in the comm rooms must lead boring lives. We could help them out."

"Don't you dare."

He chuckled. "Don't worry. I'll save the discovery fantasies for nonwork areas."

"Cooper."

"Yes?"

"Stop talking and take me. Now."

"I love it when you give orders." Gently, he pushed her back so that she could lie on the trunk of the car with her feet on the bumper. Her black skirt fell back all the way to her hips, exposing her naked thighs. "I'm only going to take your panties off."

She felt him slip them down her legs and then a soft whisper of fabric. He must have pocketed them. Then she felt his breath on her thighs. "Cooper—"

"I'm really going to look at this vehicle differently now," he said, and tongued her.

"Mmf!"

"Shh." He spread her legs apart and she felt the tickle of his hair on her thighs as he licked her again. "Don't want to wake the neighbors."

She willed herself not to cry out as that clever tongue stroked the length of her lips, teasing and arousing. Her fingertips flattened on the metal of the trunk as she tried to keep quiet. "So sweet," he crooned. "So wet for me."

And before she could scream, he found her clit and settled on it, his tongue moving in short, hard strokes as he held her spread wide on the trunk of the car.

The pleasure, oh, the pleasure, the sweet wet skill of his tongue…

Her orgasm, which had been building just beneath the surface, burst under his mouth and she made a high, keening sound in the back of her throat. The waves rolled through her, cresting and rippling out along every muscle in her body, exploding in her head and making her see light where there had been none.

Dazed, her knees weak, she slid toward him. "I need you."

She may have been weak, but his intent was clear and strong. He pulled her toward him and instinctively she wrapped her legs around his hips. In those few seconds she'd been gasping and dazzled, he'd rolled on a condom so that this hollow need inside her could be satisfied immediately.

"Yes," she sighed as her body accepted his length and he slid into her on one smooth stroke. He leaned over her, hands flat on the trunk lid on either side of her, and she pulled him tightly against her with her ankles. "That's it. Oh, yes."

It felt glorious to be filled this way, to hear his breathing speed up, to feel the tremors in his hips as they flexed and bucked against her body, to know he was losing himself in her just as she'd lost herself in him.

A guttural sound broke from his lips, quickly stifled, as his body stiffened and he surged into her one final time. A second sound, and his muscles gave out and he collapsed against her, even in his extremity making sure that she wouldn't be bumped against the hard metal.

In the dark, the only sound was their breathing as they both tried to recover.

Joanna wrapped her arms around him, marveling at the heat and strength of his body even as his back heaved with every breath. Enjoying how perfect and taut each muscle felt under her fingers.

She had to face the truth now. She hadn't broken all those rules and ignored her own principles to make herself feel better this time. She'd done it because she wanted to. Because she wanted him. Because she wanted him to see her not as a cop, but as a desirable woman.

She'd put her career at risk because she wanted to be as sexy and womanly and desirable as it was possible to be. And she'd enjoyed every second of it.

Even though it was the one thing she'd sworn years ago would never happen.

So what exactly was she going to do now?

The darkness, which they'd co-opted to make their own, had no answer.

14

COOPER SLOUCHED IN the classroom chair and surreptitiously counted heads. True to their agreement, the P.D. had hung on to Julian. Out of all the people in this class, it had been a stroke of luck that his "buddy" had been Julian Royden. Who knew how much information they'd eventually be able to squeeze out of him about Afrodita Enterprises? The guy had a lot to lose, and Cooper had no qualms about using it against him.

He'd be interested to see what Leah dug up today using the fake "support group sign-up sheet" he'd compiled yesterday. Even if some of them had only noted an e-mail address or a phone number, she could come up with names, addresses and criminal records with less. And it was the people with past records who interested them the most. After watching Darren behave like a relatively normal guy, Cooper was ready to give some credence to Joanna's theory about the Rules working best on someone with a predisposition to violence. Maybe they could narrow their net to just a few, and head off a spike in the crime rate before it got started.

Their instructor didn't bat an eye at his student's absence. He probably didn't care if Julian was there or not, as long as his check cleared. Even if the washout rate was fifty percent, who was going to ask for a refund and admit he couldn't get a date even with instructions?

"Yesterday I touched briefly on the Third Rule," Richard Benton began. "Does anyone remember what it is?"

Someone near the door read from his notes. *"The biological imperative must be served first, before values, before preferences, even before belief."* He looked up from his notebook, puzzled. "What does that mean, exactly?"

"Let's take it in pieces," Benton said. "When I say before values, I mean before commonly accepted social mores, such as modesty, courtesy and so on. Social trimmings are useless to the biological imperative. And preferences should be clear. Yes, you're going to want to enjoy sex with a beautiful woman. But if she doesn't have the big breasts you prefer, or the long legs, or the great butt, you can't let that stop you. If the woman is receptive to the interruption of her energy and the verbal cues, that's the one you want. Your urge for sex comes first, gentlemen."

Cooper waved a lazy hand. "What if she lets you interrupt her energy and she goes with the verbal cues, and then changes her mind?"

Benton shook his head. "If you're careful with your timing, as we discussed yesterday, she can't change her mind. It isn't possible."

The guy in the flannel shirt—was it the same shirt?—straightened in his seat. "I dunno about that. How many of us actually got a woman into bed last night?" He looked around the room.

Cooper smothered a smile as man after man seemed to shrink in his seat, like eight-year-olds trying to disappear before the teacher called on them for an answer they didn't have. Darren Phillips gazed out the window, a goofy smile on his lips.

"Oh, come now," Benton said. "One of you must have scored."

"I did."

"Me, too."

"Excellent." Benton beamed at the two men like an approving parent. This was so sick, Cooper thought. "So what went wrong with the rest of you?"

"She got away on me." Flannel Guy sounded injured. "We got to the end of the block and she took off. I didn't think women could run that fast in high heels."

"You didn't keep your hand on her control switch, did you?" Benton asked. "Or keep up the interruption process on her energy meridians?"

"I thought I did, but I guess not. She was awful slippery. Kept wiggling out of the way."

"The woman I picked did that, too," Cooper said. "I'm thinking it's not foolproof—that there are things she can do to escape."

"Only before the process really takes hold," Benton said impatiently. "She can evade being touched, of course. But there's no safe word that makes her immune. No meridian that she can manipulate herself to undo your work. As long as you keep within the time limits, you have the power here. The Rules are all about you."

Cooper could just imagine Leah and Joanna throwing virtual rotten vegetables at the tape deck as they heard *that*.

The rest of the day's work consisted of fine-tuning the skills of the students and familiarizing them more thoroughly with the way energy worked in the body—both male and female. While he went through the motions of working with Andrea, Cooper strategized. He needed both Joanna and Will on the streets tonight, keeping an eye on potential assault victims as his classmates tried their skills on a second "field trip." He'd invent an urgent appointment or find some other way of sliding out of the assignment so he could get out there, too.

No more baits for Joanna. If she did that, it meant Will was tied to her as her cover, and couldn't be used to help if something else came up. Joanna probably wouldn't like it as much, but he'd convince her they needed to change their plan of attack.

And if that didn't work, he'd pull rank.

JOANNA'S CELL PHONE rang just after she and Will had returned with In-N-Out burgers to go. She unwrapped her cheeseburger—animal style, with lots of cheese and broiled onions—as she cradled the phone between her shoulder and her ear.

"MacPherson."

"Investigator MacPherson, this is Nate Randall from Santa Rita P.D. We spoke briefly last night, after you interviewed Julian Royden."

"Oh, sure. How is Julian?"

"Annoyed and very vocal."

"He's a lawyer. What did we expect?"

But evidently Detective Randall wasn't in the mood

for humor. "Listen, you asked me to let you know when we had any assaults reported."

Joanna's stomach flip-flopped and she put the cheeseburger down. "You've got one?"

"Well, no. What we have is a body, discovered on the beach this morning by a surfer. But technically she was assaulted before she died. The coroner said she was raped."

"Oh, no," Joanna whispered. She cleared her throat. "What else did he say?"

"Unfortunately, there was no evidence of the rape. It washed away during her time in the water. But she has a lot of bruising that isn't consistent with bumping against a piling or anything. Finger-shaped bruising around the neck, upper arms and thighs. Fits the profile you gave me, so that's why I'm calling."

She was supposed to stick around to monitor Cooper's transmitter and learn all the nauseating ways a man could control a woman if he believed hard enough in these stupid Rules. But Leah would let her know if any earth-shattering gems fell from Richard Benton's lips.

Joanna made up her mind. "And I appreciate it. I want to have a look. Be there in fifteen minutes."

"I'll have a visitor badge ready for you at the counter."

She hung up and grabbed her handbag. "Leah, the P.D. have the body of a woman who's been assaulted."

"Body?" Leah sounded startled as she swung around, pulling off her headphones.

"Yes. A surfer found her washed up on the beach this morning. It may not have anything to do with our case, but I'm going to have a look anyway." She reached for flippancy to scrub away the image. "Maybe there'll be something in the coroner's report that relates to energy meridians."

"But what do I tell Cooper?" Leah asked. "He doesn't want you out there. You're supposed to be monitoring his class."

"I have my cell. You can let me know if anything important comes up. And don't worry about Cooper. I'll handle him."

Brave words, but they only worked on one level. As she drove downtown, Joanna was reminded with every turn of the wheel that this was the vehicle on which they'd made such fabulous, clandestine love the night before.

Just how long was she going to allow this to continue? Because if she were smart, she'd admit that it couldn't, she'd tell Cooper it couldn't, and she'd stop doing stupid things like letting him kiss her. And touch her. And turn her into a ball of melted fire that couldn't say no.

For Pete's sake, he had his own set of Rules operating, here, and she was just as helpless under them as she'd been with Thomas Semple.

Now there was a depressing thought.

Was that all desire was? A way to make it easy for the male to have his way with the female, even though she knew it was against her own best interests?

There was a reason for her personal rule against on-the-job relationships. She'd seen the odd look Leah had given her when she'd finally come in. Leah wasn't stupid—and it didn't take twenty minutes to park a car. She had to suspect that something was going on, but Joanna was certainly not the one to enlighten her. Just let that get back to Bella and her hopes of having the

Bling incident struck from her personnel file were slim to none.

You can't afford any more mistakes.

CLEU's recruitment standards were set high—which was why it had meant so much to her to be tapped for a spot in the L.A. unit. The look on her dad's face when she'd told him about it and what such a move meant had been worth it. How would he feel if it got back to him that she'd lost her job because she had poor impulse control? Or because she'd let her libido control her intellect?

That look she hated—that look that said, "You're just a girl. Your job is to look pretty and get married," would seep back into his eyes and she'd spend the next twenty years trying to erase it.

Unthinkable.

Why do you care what he thinks? Live the life you love, not the one you think he'll love.

But no matter what she told herself, she couldn't stop caring what Admiral Reg MacPherson thought. She couldn't erase the memory of being six and landing the part of a mouse in the school play and rushing home to tell him about it—only to find him off watching her brothers play soccer. Or of being chosen to play defense on the girls' team in junior high and having him shrug it off as "girls' soccer. Who watches that?"

It was only when she graduated with a degree in justice administration and was accepted into the L.A.P.D.'s training academy that he finally looked at her as if he saw her—her, not a pale shadow of the man he wished she was.

Now he treated her like—well, like one of her brothers, as an equal. Someone who had something to contribute, not someone who supported and cooked for and ironed the shirts of people who contributed. Joanna often wondered how her mother stood it. But when she'd asked one time, Mom had just shrugged and said she was from a different generation—and happy enough not to be out there competing the way Joanna did.

Conscious that she hadn't really made a decision, and equally conscious that she needed to before she was alone with Cooper again, Joanna pulled into the city lot behind the Santa Rita Police Department's headquarters. A badge waited for her at the desk, and the reception clerk buzzed her through once she had it clipped to the lapel of her white shirt.

She found Nate Randall at his desk. He shut down what looked like a case report and stood. "Investigator," he greeted her as he shook hands.

"Please. Everyone calls me Joanna."

"Okay, Joanna. You ready? Our victim is over at the county morgue around the corner."

Fifteen minutes later she and Nate waited as the pathologist, whose name tag said Tran Vu, M.D., rolled the body out and uncovered her. Joanna sucked in a breath.

Nate looked at her curiously. "Something wrong?"

"I know her."

"Know her?" the pathologist repeated sharply. "Can you give us an ID?"

Joanna's lungs felt as though someone were squeezing them. She struggled to keep her breathing steady as she catalogued the litany of bruises that told the story of what had happened to this girl before she died. The poor kid still wore the burgundy party dress…though the chiffon overskirt had been torn away, probably by rocks or gravel.

"I was at the Pink Salamander on Saturday night, and we shared a mirror in the bathroom. Her first name is Danielle. I didn't get a last name. She just graduated from UC Santa Rita and landed a job at Starfish Software." Joanna swallowed the lump in her throat. "That's why she was out at the club. She was celebrating her new job."

Nate pulled out his notebook and took a few notes. "So if I called HR over at Starfish, they'd have a record of her?"

"A record…a job application…references. Next of kin. So you can at least notify her family."

Dr. Vu nodded. "We'll get a positive ID from them. Thank you. You've been very helpful. What was it you were looking for, anyway?"

"Could you turn her over, please?"

Carefully, the pathologist did so. "Something in particular?"

Joanna nodded. *Breathe in. Out. Stay professional. Don't break down.* "See that mottling between her shoulder blades?"

"That mean something?" Nate asked.

"It means Danielle probably had a run-in with someone using these Rules of Seduction we're investigating." Anger began a slow boil under her breastbone. She could handle that much better than the grief that a life with such happiness and potential could be cut short so brutally. She would never see Danielle's name in the credits now.

"These what?" The pathologist stared at her, completely at sea.

Joanna filled him in on the investigation. Then she

indicated the bruising on Danielle's back. "I understand that this area here is what they call the 'control switch.' I'm thinking the perpetrator got impatient and started hitting the switch too hard. And then he got completely carried away when it didn't work."

"You're really serious, aren't you?" Dr. Vu said.

"I'm afraid so," Nate put in. "It's serious. Weird, but serious."

"There's a spike in crimes against persons in every city where these workshops are held," Joanna told them. She watched Dr. Vu turn Danielle over and cover her up again. "I just wish we'd been able to stop this one. I didn't realize it would progress to murder."

"You think he meant to kill her?" Nate asked. "It could have been accidental."

"Possibly," she said. "But we still need to treat it as a homicide."

"Just what we need," the pathologist sighed. "More crazies."

"Let's hope it ends here," Nate said grimly. "Joanna, do you have all you need?"

All she needed, yes. But not all she wanted.

She thanked Nate and Dr. Vu and headed back to the car. First thing on the agenda was to huddle with Cooper and the team. Maybe Danielle was an isolated incident. But maybe the killer would strike again. If so, they needed to change their plan—before someone else wound up lying on a cold metal tray.

15

WHEN COOPER OPENED the front door after the workshop ended, Joanna was slouched in her chair in the comm room with her headphones on, looking as though she'd been there monitoring his wire all afternoon. She'd had just enough time to zip through the hour or so of tape she'd missed in order to bring herself up to date.

Now all she had to do was wait for their briefing session to tell them what she'd learned at the morgue. Homicide turned up the heat on this case—as well as the visibility. If she could nail the person who had killed Danielle, she'd be free and clear with Internal Affairs, and maybe even get on the fast track to the homicide unit.

Cooper put two pizza boxes on the table. "You guys ready to debrief?"

Leah glanced at Joanna as she pulled her own headphones off. "Be right there." She gathered a stack of sheets from the laser printer and the two women joined Cooper and Will in the kitchen.

"Here are the hits I was able to get from your support group sign-up sheet." Leah pushed them across the table to Cooper and helped herself to a slice of pizza. "Most of these guys are clean, but two of them have records—one for possession of an illegal firearm and one for assault, for which he got a suspended sentence."

"Arthur Michael Schott," Cooper said. "He sat in the row next to me—Flannel Guy. Charged with assault sixteen months ago. I'd say we watch him tonight. He seemed pretty pissed that he couldn't get the Rules to work. He might go for the direct physical approach on his field trip tonight."

"How did you get out of it?" Will asked around a mouthful of tomato and basil.

"I said I had to go back to work to make up for the time I was in class." Cooper shrugged. "What's it to them? The only place I'll ever see any of them again is in court. So. Here's the battle plan for tonight."

"I have new information," Joanna said.

"Yeah?" Cooper pushed the rap sheets aside. "Let's hear it."

From his tone, you'd never think they'd even met before, much less had an explosive orgasm on the trunk of a car. But she had to admit they needed to play it that way, especially now that the stakes had just gone up.

"I got a call from the P.D. this morning. The body of a young woman in her early twenties washed up on the beach. A surfer found her. Because I'd asked to be alerted if any assaults were reported, they called me once the coroner's people determined she actually had been assaulted."

Cooper's eyes had narrowed with a frown. "How did they know it was homicide?"

"Seemed pretty clear. There are finger- and hand-shaped bruises all over her."

"But how can you link that to our case?" Will wanted to know.

"First, because a number of those bruises were clustered in the control button area," Joanna said quietly.

"And second?" Cooper prompted.

"And second, because I met her Saturday night. In the restroom at the Pink Salamander. Her name was Danielle."

"Oh, no," Leah breathed.

Joanna went on, "She was there celebrating a new job, so the P.D. is going to contact her new employer to find out her last name and next of kin."

"You knew that?" Will said.

Joanna shrugged. "Women talk in the bathroom. She was so excited and so bubbly that she probably over-shared, which may have gotten her into trouble when the perpetrator approached her."

Cooper got up, raking a hand through his hair. "This is bigger than bait-and-catches now. We need to call in the troops, and partner with the local detectives to find this guy before he goes after someone else."

"No, we can't," Joanna said. "If we bring in the locals, they're bound to be recognized by someone. That could tip him off that we're investigating."

"Joanna, none of us is qualified to run a homicide investigation—unless you've had a promotion lately we don't know about."

Somehow she had to convince him that they could do it. "Of course not. I know we haven't been through the academy modules and all that stuff, but we're street-smart. And this is still a crimes against persons case. If we—"

"No," Cooper said flatly. "Even if we were on the homicide team, we don't have the resources to do it ourselves. Three people can't go up against the whole town. We need the P.D.'s personnel, we need their lab—we need their cooperation, period. If this has escalated, there's going to be a turf war and you know it."

"Nobody was talking turf war when I was at the morgue this afternoon. They were handling it as part of their normal case load—the detective only called me as a courtesy. As far as they're concerned, it's unrelated to our investigation because there's no physical link. A cluster of bruises isn't enough to form a joint forces operation on."

Cooper sat back and studied her face. "So this whole conversation is moot, then. We let the P.D. handle the homicide and we concentrate on the assaults, the way our brief says."

"But it is connected," she insisted. "You know it and I know it, even though we can't prove it so it'll stand up in court. That has to change the way we operate."

"We can't go out there hoping we can stop this with baits," Will agreed. "That'd be like standing with a finger in the dam, plugging one hole while water is spurting out all over."

Joanna threw him a grateful glance. It was about time someone spoke up to support her point of view.

"That's all we can do at the moment." The frown was back between Cooper's eyes.

How did he handle pressure? Joanna wondered. As team lead, was he used to having people obey orders without question, or did he ask for a consensus before he went ahead? He'd been supportive of her methods—unconventional though they were sometimes—up to this point. Would that stop here and now, when she disagreed with him in front of the junior investigators?

"We let the P.D. have the homicide and act in a support capacity with these assaults until we can find a link." Cooper folded up the pizza boxes and put them in the trash, as though the conversation was over.

"I have a suggestion," Joanna said.

"Yeah?" He didn't look as if he cared much, but he pulled out the kitchen chair and sat anyway.

"Remember Tracey Bigelow, the victim I interviewed? She had red hair. So did poor Danielle. What if our killer has a thing for redheads?" She looked at Cooper, Will and Leah in turn. "I propose that I go out there and try to lure him in."

"Absolutely not," Cooper pushed his chair back and got up. "Come on, let's get—"

"Listen to me for a second." Joanna pushed her own chair back, and the two of them faced off over the Formica tabletop. "You're the psychologist, right? You tell me whether two assaults on women with similar builds and coloring could be the basis of a profile."

"That's not how it works, Joanna." His gaze intensified and focused with warning. "You form a profile from the signature a killer leaves at the scene. We don't have a crime scene—we don't even have physical evidence to tie anybody to the body. You can't walk out there and assume that because two random redheads were attacked that suddenly we have a serial killer on our hands."

"Even if we might?"

He took a long breath, as if to calm his temper. "Even if we did, we need evidence. We need time. We need manpower. None of which we've got right now."

"What we have is a redhead beaten up on Friday night, and a redhead killed on Saturday night," she reminded him. "What if he holds to his pattern and there's a redhead assaulted or killed tomorrow night? Will that be enough evidence for you?"

"I think you're jumping to conclusions."

"Well, I don't. Half of this job is going by your gut, and my gut tells me we need to move. Tonight."

"From what I hear, your gut isn't all that reliable," he said in a tone that could freeze the water in the pipes.

Will and Leah looked at each other, came to some unspoken agreement and slowly faded out of the room. Joanna barely saw them go.

"What's that supposed to mean?"

"Nothing."

"It isn't nothing. What did you hear? From whom?"

He shrugged and shoved his hands deep into his pockets. "I heard somewhere that you're prone to go off suddenly and break the rules. I'm thinking this is part of your pattern."

"My pattern. What, are you profiling me now, instead of this guy who hates redheads?"

"No, but you have to admit your temper makes you do things you're sorry for."

"Anthony Bingham has nothing to do with this case. And I'm sorry I ever told you about him."

"I never said he did. But you can't get all fired up and hit the streets half-cocked. That's a sure way to get yourself—and your team—into trouble."

"You're mixing your gun metaphors."

"And you're evading my point."

"And what's that? That you're the boss and no matter what my instincts tell me, we have to do what you say?"

"I'm the team lead, and we decide what to do together."

"Bull. You've decided my theory is crap, so you're going to be a good boy and play by the P.D.'s rules. No interference, no turf wars, keep everything nice and cozy. Meantime, maybe another girl gets beaten to death."

"Okay, that's it." Cooper lifted his hands in a gesture that might have meant surrender in any other man, but managed to convey the impression that he was washing his hands of her. "You're angry and getting personal. Take some time to calm down and we'll talk about strategy again later."

"Don't you walk out on me," she warned. "I'm not finished."

"If you don't settle down and work this out, you might be." His tone was calm, but she could tell he struggled to keep it that way.

What was the matter with her? Why was she pushing him so hard? It wasn't like he was out of line. His reasoning was sound, but that didn't mean she had to like it. All of a sudden it seemed that he was stepping onto the side of every other man in authority who had ever taken her ideas and tossed them out, just because she was a woman. If Will had broached this theory about the redheads, would he have listened?

"Now what are you talking about?" she snapped.

"How many chances do you have left before CLEU tosses you out?" he demanded. "Huh? How many more mistakes have to be expunged from your record before you—"

He stopped, and she felt the blood drain from her face.

"I never told you that," she whispered. "Did Bella say that?"

He turned away, shaking his head.

"You've read my file." The discovery rocked her back, and she found herself up against the refrigerator. "How did you get permission to do that?" Still no answer. "Bella would never give you access, and your lieutenant can't bring up other units' records. How did you know about expunging Bling from my record?"

When he didn't reply, she crashed into the only conclusion she had left.

"You hacked into the system, didn't you? Or had someone do it for you." When he sucked on his lower lip—as she'd done herself the other night—and said nothing, she knew she was right. "Well, I hope you found what you wanted. I hope you feel all-powerful now, knowing all about me while I know next to nothing about you."

"That's not it," he said.

"Really. Enlighten me."

"For God's sake, Joanna, I'm sorry, all right?" Hot blood washed into his face and some immature part of her was glad that at last she'd gotten a reaction out of him. The more rational part of her felt uncomfortably aware that she was pushing—pushing—and she might push him away altogether.

But did it stop her? No.

In fact, it would be better if she did push him away. Both professionally and personally.

"No, you're not."

"I'm sorry I breached your confidence. But I wanted to know what kind of partner I was working with. I wanted to be sure you—we—"

"You wanted to be sure I wouldn't screw it up, is that what you're trying to say?"

"No. Yes."

He thought she'd fail and yet he'd stepped outside the careful boundaries that the regulations had created for them and made love to her anyway. Why? Because he'd rather relate to her as a woman, as a sex partner, than as a fellow officer?

"Is that how you feel about us, too, Cooper?" She dropped her voice to a whisper. "I hope you have more confidence in my abilities in bed than on the street."

Emotion flickered across his face, making him drop his lashes to hide his eyes from her. He turned away. "You don't need to get personal."

"You got personal the minute you broke into my file. This whole thing is personal. Well, let me tell you something, Cooper Maxwell. The only reason anything happened on that sailboat was because I wanted it to. I needed to prove to myself that the Rules had worn off, that I was still normal, and you were handy. Don't read anything personal into *that,* because it wasn't. It was strictly medicinal. Nothing more."

He turned his head away, but not before she saw the hot color of emotion fade to the cold paleness of hurt. Pushing the back door open, he went out into the yard and closed it carefully behind him.

And in that quiet sound, Joanna heard the end of the heat between them. The end of the laughter.

And the end of all possibility that these feelings inside her, this respect, this need, would ever be satisfied by him again.

16

144 Vista Mar
Santa Rita, California
22:08 hours

"If I were a guy, I'd pick you up."

Will got out of their unmarked vehicle and went around to the passenger door to let Joanna out.

"Weren't you a guy the last time you checked?"

A beat too late, he realized what he'd said, and his shaggy surfer hair fell forward as his cheeks turned scarlet. "I meant a guy on the street," he mumbled. "You know what I mean."

With a laugh, she tugged on his hand and they strolled down the main drag, looking like new acquaintances enjoying the summer evening. That wasn't so far off, either. The bitter knowledge that she'd made a mistake in pushing Cooper away was a bad taste in her mouth. The certainty that she and Will had disobeyed a direct order in coming out on their own had agitated butterflies swooping and flittering in her stomach.

But they were committed now. Cooper had gone out. She didn't know where, but she hoped she wouldn't see him in one of these clubs, hooking up with some sweet young thing who wouldn't carp at him and thwart him and disappoint him. Leah, dedicated but cautious, had agreed to give them radio support, even though Cooper's departure had given them all tacit permission to take the night off.

"Where are we going to start?" Will asked. "We haven't paid much attention to Atlantis."

"But Tracey and Danielle were both last seen at the Pink Salamander. I think we should start there."

"Suits me. I'll go in first and let you know the situation."

The pounding bass of a live performance at the Salamander reverberated in Joanna's gut as she loitered on the street, looking in the window of a clothing boutique that obviously catered to the college crowd. Way too much black. In a few minutes, Leah's voice sounded quietly in her ear.

"Joanna, Will reports that the Pink Salamander is crowded because of the band. You won't get a seat at the bar, but there are a lot of people standing near the windows, particularly men. He's there now. He recommends you join them and he'll shadow you."

"Copy that," Joanna said. "I'm going in now."

She crossed the street and pushed open the Salamander's door. The music practically made her hair blow back—or maybe that was the welcoming blast of air-conditioning. In any case, it took a few minutes to secure a drink, and then she wound her way through the tables and past dancing couples to the crowd standing near the windows.

A smile tilted one side of her mouth as she saw Will gamely fending off the advances of a pair of college girls dressed to the teeth and ready to party. She herself had dressed carefully. Danielle had been wearing a very feminine outfit. Maybe it had nothing to do with their target's taste, but on the off chance that it did, Joanna had chosen a ruffled chiffon sleeveless shirt over a short flowered skirt. So not her usual style, but Leah had been sweet to lend it to her. She'd undone the first couple of buttons and fastened a fake pearl necklace around her throat.

As she sipped her drink and tapped a foot in time to the music, a man with brown hair dressed in a business suit with the tie loosened asked her to dance. It didn't take long to figure out that he didn't know the Rules from a parking ticket, and besides, the hip gyrations were downright embarrassing.

She ditched him after the song ended and caught Will's eye. With a nod toward the ladies' room, she began to move in that direction. It was kind of cute to see him try to disengage from the college girls in order to shadow her. Technically he didn't have to, but the kid was serious about his job.

There were only a couple of women in line, so she chatted with them, making jokes about the band and the crowd, complimenting one on her hair and the other on her necklace.

Then she said, "Did y'all hear about the crime problem they're having around here? Scary, isn't it?"

The women looked at her curiously. "What do you mean?" one of them said, then went into a cubicle. "Keep talking, I'm listening."

"There's this thing where guys try to touch you on your shoulder, wrist, or here—" she demonstrated

"—between your shoulder blades. They mess with your body energy somehow and say a code word, and before you know it, you're Zombie Girl and they can do whatever they want to."

"What?"

"Girl, you're certified nuts."

"Seriously," Joanna protested. "It happened to me on Saturday. But I got lucky—a friend came in and stopped me as I was leaving with this guy I'd never seen before in my life. Totally didn't know what was going on, but luckily for me, he didn't have to. So, yeah, pass it on. Tell your friends to watch out for guys touching those three places."

"Weird," the two girls agreed as they slipped out the restroom door, looking at Joanna over their shoulders.

She wasn't sure if they meant her or her warning, but at least she'd done what she could. When she came out, the line extended down the corridor. She repeated her warning in the most charming and cordial way she could. If only one girl was able to escape one of these guys and his damn biological imperative, she'd sleep easier at night. With a smile and a request for them all to pass it on, she stopped near the pay phone. Surveying the crowd, she tried to pick out the geeks and losers. Was it the fact that she was chasing thirty that nearly everyone looked like a geek or a loser to her?

Or, face it, are you comparing these guys to Cooper and they're coming up short?

Now, there was a pointless train of thought, guaranteed to make her jump the track of her mission here. She couldn't afford to be distracted by longing, or the memories of the way he closed his eyes in ecstasy and the tendons in his neck stretched as he tried to keep from crying out. At the very thought, a dart of desire flashed through her and her body softened and moistened in response.

Why, why, why had she been so stupid and so weak? Now he'd haunt her for weeks, teasing her with memory, as though he'd imprinted himself in her cells and they were all waiting for him to come back.

Well, they'd have to wait. She'd made her decision and she couldn't go back now—couldn't admit that she felt like a crumb for hurting him. Couldn't confess that all she'd wanted to do the previous evening was to run out into the backyard, under the darkness of that tree out there, and ask him to forgive her for the things she'd said.

Too late now. That moment of opportunity would never come again. And disobeying his orders would put a permanent rift between them. She'd never be able to mend it even if they were tapped to work together again after this.

The only comfort she had was her gut feeling that, as far as these girls downtown were concerned, she was doing the right thing. Someone had to step into the breach for them, and she was the only one who could.

Cold comfort, maybe, but in law enforcement, putting the job ahead of your own feelings was what you did.

"Enjoying the music?"

Joanna turned, jolted out of her unhappy musings. A man in his early forties stood next to her, having obviously come out of the men's room at the opposite end of the corridor. He looked like a successful middle manager, with dark hair going silver at the temples, and a trim build that suggested regular workouts.

"I've never heard the band before," she said. "Are they local?"

He nodded. "They play the clubs here a lot. I've got a couple of their CDs."

Middle age was stalking him, so he was evidently doing his best to ward it off by listening to bands whose demographics were at least ten years younger, wearing cargo pants and a linen jacket instead of a suit. Joanna bet herself ten bucks that there was a red Corvette in a parking lot somewhere, too, and maybe a divorce lawyer with a recent couple of thousand in his pocket.

"Would you like to dance?" he asked.

Why not? She could scope the crowd as easily from the dance floor as from here, and it would be easier for Will to keep an eye on her. "Sure. How about the—"

"There's a private lounge through here." He indicated the hallway behind him. "It's upstairs, so you can hear the music and see the band, but it's not so crowded."

She smiled. "Do you have special privileges or what?"

He shrugged modestly. "They know me here."

Leah would transmit her location to Will, so she'd be safe. "Okay, let's go." She tucked her evening clutch under her arm and followed him down the hall to an unmarked door.

He opened it and stood aside to let her pass, and she found herself in a hallway lit by a single recessed light. "Just through there. We have to go behind the bar before we get to the stairs."

She hadn't noticed a second floor, but that wasn't surprising, with all of them focusing on the people in the place, not the architecture. Sure enough, a set of stairs led upward to another door. The scent of his cologne reached her nose as she leaned on the handle, and then two things happened at once.

She opened the door, not onto a private lounge, but onto the alley behind the club.

And the man's hand settled between her shoulder blades, where her muscles involuntarily contracted with the knowledge that she'd just made the worst mistake of all.

COOPER HAD LIVED in California all his life, but for some reason his trips to the beach had been few and far between. Of course, growing up in Lodi had meant that, outside of the occasional summer vacation, the closest he'd been able to get to water was the irrigation ditches that crisscrossed the acres of fruit trees and fields. And after the death of his parents and his and his sister's abrupt and unwelcome entry into the foster care system, there had been no trips to the beach. Just survival, plain and simple, until the day he turned eighteen and they cut him loose.

He slouched in the driver's seat of the second of the team's unmarked vehicles. Through the open window, he heard the slow, rhythmic boom and whisper of the combers, like a giant's heartbeat against the chest of the world.

He had hoped to find some mental peace and quiet, but the auto-replay in his head just wouldn't shut up. Wouldn't turn off the sound of Joanna's voice. Wouldn't blank out the expression in her eyes when she realized he was going to let red tape wrap around their investigation and choke off her plan.

But what other choice did he have? He knew she operated on the fly, and in some circumstances that could be a good thing. But when you added homicide to the mix, you had to act carefully. You had to bring in help. You had to assist the locals, not antagonize them.

So here he was, trying to find a measure of calm before he drove over to the P.D. and offered their assistance in the investigation. Joanna would pitch a fit. She wanted to keep their unit small and nimble and under the radar. But she wasn't running this show. He'd been around the block enough times to know that sometimes you had to give in and admit that your unit needed help. In this case, it was mutual. They could help the P.D. and the P.D. could help them.

Decision made, he started the car and rolled up the window. Police headquarters was downtown, a block or so off the main drag, but Santa Rita was so small it didn't take long to get there. He flashed his shield at the counter and asked for Nate Randall.

"He's not in," the clerk at the window said. "He works days."

"What about anyone else working on the girl who washed up on the beach yesterday?"

"Oh." The clerk picked up the phone. "Nate wanted to be called if anything came in on that one. Let me see what he wants to do."

As it turned out, despite the lateness of the hour, Nate was more than happy to meet him at a coffee bar close to his neighborhood. Cooper shook his hand and slid onto a stool at the far end of the place while Nate got a couple of steaming cups for them both.

"I met your partner earlier," he said, taking the stool

opposite. "She gave me a couple of days' jump on identifying our victim. I appreciate that."

"Did you get a positive ID?" Cooper asked.

"Danielle Starkweather, aged twenty-three, from Boise, Idaho. She went through UC Santa Rita on a scholarship and planned to stay once she landed the job at Starfish. Needless to say, her parents are devastated."

"Boyfriend? Anyone who disliked her?"

"Not according to her roommate, who was also at the club that night." He held up a hand. "And before you ask, no, she didn't see a thing. She went home with an upset stomach shortly after your partner bumped into them in the ladies' room, and didn't see who Danielle hooked up with."

"Too bad she didn't take her roommate home," Cooper observed.

"Luck of the draw. One of their other friends gave her a lift."

"So nobody saw anything."

"Not that we've been able to determine yet. We're still working on the staff at the Salamander, showing her picture and hoping somebody remembers her. Like I say, having your partner give us a partial ID so fast could really make a difference."

"That's partly what I wanted to talk with you about. Joanna is convinced we have a serial killer on our hands."

Nate blinked, and took a sip of coffee, as if his mouth had suddenly gone dry. "What makes her think so?"

Cooper shook his head. "It seems pretty insubstantial to me, but an assault victim she interviewed on Sunday had red hair. So did your victim."

Nate waited. "That's it?"

"Yeah. The problem is, she's convinced that if she continues with the bait-and-snatches we've been doing, she might flush him out."

"Why does she—oh, I get it. Red hair. So what are you going to do?"

Cooper shifted and gazed out the window at the darkened street. Other than the lights of the coffee bar and the convenience store next to it, this neighborhood was dark. People slept safely in their houses, unaware that Danielle Starkweather wasn't going to start work this week, or that Tracey Bigelow had been released the day before. They thought their streets were safe.

It was their job to make them that way, but of all their choices, which was the best one?

"I don't have enough evidence yet to ask for a joint forces operation, but that's what I want." He glanced at Nate Randall for his reaction.

Conscious that they were the only people in the place aside from two teenagers at the far end, Nate nodded and kept his voice low. "I'd welcome the help, but like you say, we don't have any evidence. But in case MacPherson turns out to be right and we do have a serial, I'll ask the lab to put a rush on the trace from Danielle's body. We might be able to match fibers or fluids, though chances of that are pretty slim. The ocean did a pretty good job of erasing anything helpful."

"I appreciate that." Cooper paused. "Anything new from our friend Julian Royden?"

Nate shrugged. "We released him. He'll appear next week on the assault charge, but we dropped the attempted rape at MacPherson's request. He'll probably get a fine and go on his merry way."

"Did he give up anything new on Afrodita Enterprises?"

"Just that the addresses given for the members of the board are all fake. He gave us the real ones."

"What, does the guy have this stuff in his pocket or what?"

"Photographic memory, apparently. I'll e-mail them to you, if you want. MacPherson has a connection with one of them. She might be interested."

Cooper stood and drained his cup, then turned to pitch it in the trash. "Thanks for meeting with me on short notice. We'll keep our eyes open."

"Likewise. You have my cell number?"

Cooper patted his pockets and remembered his own phone was back at the house, charging. He found a pen and wrote Nate's number on a napkin. Not that he had a whole lot of need for it, but you never knew. He'd been wrong before.

Cooper's neighborhood lay on the east side, which meant he had to go through downtown to get back to the safe house. The place was alive with people going in and out of the bars and restaurants, with music blasting out into the street every time someone opened a door. Half his mind focused on watching couples strolling down the avenue as he moved slowly with the traffic, and half wondered what he was going to do about Joanna.

Nothing, if she had her way. She'd been all too emphatic about that.

So what was the matter with him that he couldn't just

walk away? He'd done that plenty of times. In fact, until Kellan Black had fallen for Linn Nichols, their tight band of brothers in narcotics had had quite the rep for keeping their relationships short-term. One of his girlfriends had once told him the female investigators called him, Danny, Kell and "Slim" Jim Macormick the Fly-By Four. In other words, don't bother packing a toothbrush—you weren't going to stay.

And he'd been fine with that. Happy, even. He liked women of all shapes and sizes, though the long, leggy type like Joanna was his favorite. He'd been satisfied to enjoy their enthusiasm in bed and their companionship the rest of the time, and when it was time to move on, he'd give them a kiss and a "stay safe" and that would be that.

So what was up with him tonight? Why couldn't he crack a smile and shrug and get on with the job? She'd meant to hurt him with the "I'm just using you to make sure all my buttons still work" speech. But oddly, he couldn't blame her for that. He'd probably have done the same—gone out and found the first woman he clicked with and taken her to a hotel. But the second time they'd made love? Now, that was different, and no matter what she said, they both knew it. That had been pure, sizzling need. Need that couldn't wait to be satisfied—rooted in sexual awareness that crackled between them whenever they got within sight of each other.

She sure as hell couldn't say that was fallout from the Rules.

He knew she had problems with authority figures, but he didn't see himself in that kind of role. Her ideas were as valid as his own, and except for her plan to put herself out there as bait, he could act on them without a problem. He supposed he was an anomaly at CLEU— the guy whose strength lay in forming teams, not leading them. He'd leave that to Kellan and Danny. Kell was happy with the new stripe on the shoulder of his dress uniform, happy to lead and train and be the boss. And he was good at it, too. But Cooper was an observer of human behavior, a facilitator—skills that were probably rooted in his chaotic childhood. Maybe his ability to get teams working together was another way to form small quasi-families. Maybe that was how he coped with the lack of his own.

He was thinking over this bit of insight when the radio popped.

"Vista Base to Cooper. You on the air?"

He reached over and picked up the microphone from where it hung on its clip on the dash. "Go, Leah."

"I've been trying to raise you for half an hour. Where's your cell?"

"I left it on the charger, since we've got nothing going tonight. What's up?"

"What's your twenty?" she asked instead, and he heard the tension in her voice. Uneasiness blossomed in his belly and his grip on the microphone tightened.

"Two blocks from the house. You better tell me what's going on." He pressed the accelerator down.

"We've got trouble. Joanna took Will out on a bait and—"

"What?"

"And he just called in. He needs help."

Cooper shelved his irritation that they'd gone out

without approval and stuck with the situation at hand. "Why?"

"He's at the Pink Salamander. Joanna went to the ladies' room twenty minutes ago and never came back."

17

TWO THINGS WERE absolutely certain: One, she had been dangerously, unbelievably stupid. And two, the next time he touched her between the shoulder blades, she was done for.

Beyond those two facts, Joanna couldn't see. In fact, she couldn't see much of anything, since she was lying in the backseat of a moving car with her ankles and wrists secured with what felt like duct tape. She'd probably have a good-size goose egg on her head from where he'd clocked her.

Returning that favor was at the top of her list.

But first she had to find out where she was. And then free herself.

If she tilted her head slightly, she could get a look out the passenger window. From her acute angle, the top quarters of buildings that weren't houses scrolled past, and every block or so they paused, presumably for stop signs. So, did Santa Rita have a warehouse district? Or had she been out for hours and he'd taken her halfway to Sacramento?

They paused again and behind the stop sign she glimpsed the name of a street. Casitas. Okay, but in what city?

Use your senses.

If only it were daytime. There was a big difference between hearing the cries of seabirds and those of, say, crows or pigeons.

What do you smell?

Upholstery. New car smell. Clean floor mats with the BMW insignia.

He drove a new BMW. That meant she could get a plate number when they stopped, and an ID.

What else? His window's open.

Creosote. Salt water and kelp. Diesel fuel.

They were in the warehouse district, probably still in Santa Rita. Okay, so help was close at hand if she could find a way to contact the safe house. Will would have raised the alarm long ago. The team was probably at the Pink Salamander now, canvassing the place and showing her picture to everyone.

Surely someone, somewhere would have seen them leave. A guy couldn't pop a woman on the side of the head, tape her up and stuff her in his car without someone noticing it, could he?

Tape.

My God, am I still wearing the transmitter? Please, please, please, let him not have found it.

In an enormous stroke of luck, he'd taped her hands in front of her rather than behind. But with her wrists immobile, she could only bend at the elbows. She couldn't turn her hands to touch her ribs and feel the tiny bump of the microphone. Moving so slowly it was hardly perceptible, she tried to feel it with her forearms, but in her cramped position, it didn't work. Besides, if he saw her moving he'd know she was awake, and she wanted to play possum as long as she could.

But there was another way. Quietly, she inhaled, and the white sports-medicine tape that Leah had wrapped around her middle tightened, like the reassuring hug of a friend.

Joanna sagged with relief and let her breath out in a slow exhalation. If the tape was still there, chances were good that the transmitter was, too. All she had to do now was talk, and Leah would be able to get the information to Will and Cooper.

So, should she pretend to wake up and get the guy talking? Or should she stay motionless and hope she could surprise him and escape? Though it was pretty hard to surprise anybody when your kickboxing legs were taped together.

The depth of her predicament began to sink in in a serious way. Lying in the backseat of a crazy's BMW, with who knew what kind of treatment ahead of her in the next hour, Joanna was forced to admit that without the ability to get physical, she was as helpless as a trussed-up chicken.

The fact was, she wasn't a team player. Her sergeant knew it, her lieutenant knew it, and she hadn't been willing to admit it because, damn it, she knew she had to play nice if she was going to succeed. Except that hadn't gone all that well, either. She'd been too used to trusting only herself, and using her physical abilities to get herself out of tight situations that a person who had used her head wouldn't have been in in the first place. And what had that got her?

A prime view of a floor mat and a hundred percent probability that she was going to wind up looking like Tracey Bigelow.

Best case.

Worst case? She'd wash up on the beach a couple of days from now. At least Dr. Vu down there at the morgue would have no trouble identifying her.

For the first time, Joanna questioned her own methods. Why did she do it? Was she trying to play rough and tough, like her brothers or a true daughter of Reg MacPherson? Or was it something less admirable than that? Did she behave this way because it gave her the chance to thumb her nose at authority? Was she going "nah nah nah" at the male-oriented hierarchy at CLEU because the whole shooting match was a stand-in for her dad?

I love my dad.

You love to please him, you mean. You love to have his approval. And when you can't get it by being yourself, you get it by being some kind of kick-butt troublemaker who gets all the wrong kind of recognition.

Joanna, you need serious therapy if you ever hope to have a career.

She'd ditched her team to be what her lieutenant called a "cowboy"—a loose cannon, out of control— and now she was going to pay for it. All she could hope for was that her team hadn't ditched her in return—that Cooper was looking for her.

Now that she'd let herself think about him, the pain and regret for the things she'd said and the way she'd ignored his wishes threatened to swamp her. She couldn't afford to break down. She had to be strong and alert and smart—three things that had been woefully missing so far this evening.

She couldn't rely on her physical ability. She couldn't rely on her environment. The only things on her side right now were the transmitter and her belief in Cooper's investigative skills.

And if one of those two went missing, she'd be in deep shit.

Joanna's weight sagged forward and she realized that her captor had applied the brakes, and not to coast through a stop sign, either. She resisted correcting the dip of her body and let inertia roll her back to her initial position. The car slid from darkness punctuated by the artificial orange glow of the street lamps and the bright night lights on the warehouses into a deeper darkness. One that made the quiet purr of the Beemer's engine echo. Like a bat, she waited for the sound to bounce off the walls and tell her what kind of space they were in.

It had to be a warehouse. A big empty one, two pauses for stop signs in an unidentified direction from a street called Casitas. The team should be able to work with that.

He opened his door and got out, the car sagging to the left and back again. He slammed the door.

"Leah," she said urgently, "I'm in a warehouse two blocks from—"

The passenger door opened. "You're awake, I see," he said.

So much for the element of surprise.

"That didn't take long. I'll obviously have to work harder. Get out."

"I can't. You taped my feet," she said.

"I'm not as trusting as you. Get out."

"Where are we?"

"It doesn't matter."

When she didn't move, he sighed. "Fine. Be difficult. But I don't want to hear a sound out of you, or I'll tape your mouth, too. I've got plenty left on the roll."

He reached into the car and grabbed her by the shoulders, hauling her up and out. With all her strength, she swung both fists at his face.

As if he'd been expecting her to fight back, he ducked and her blow went wild. "Nasty, nasty," he said, drawing his *A*s out as if he were mimicking some fancy British accent. She had a moment of déjà vu. Somebody else did that. Someone she'd heard recently. Then every other thought was erased as he used her own momentum to drop her to the ground, where her head clunked on the filthy concrete.

She clawed her way out of a dizzying cloud of black spots. "Casitas!" she shouted. "Casitas!"

"Shut up, you silly girl. I meant it about the tape." He paused, and she saw that her ruffled, feminine blouse had pulled apart in the struggle. A button rolled away on the concrete in the sudden silence. "What's this?"

With a yank, he ripped the blouse open all the way, exposing the band of white tape, the transmitter bulb and its tiny power supply.

For a second, he stared at it and Joanna grabbed her opportunity. In a move that would have made some break-dancer proud, she spun on one shoulder and swung her taped-together feet at his head. But the guy must either be really good at subduing the women who fought back, or he'd had combat training, because he blocked the blow with one hand and pushed her over onto her face.

Her breasts ground painfully into the concrete, but it wasn't half as painful as what happened when he ripped the tape off her skin. She swore and tried to swing her feet at him a second time, but he evaded them and planted one buffed leather loafer in the small of her back while he smashed the transmitter with the other.

The breath whooshed out of her as he put his entire weight on her as casually as if she were a sidewalk or a stair, and not a human being. But then, the guy was clearly a psychopath, and she doubted he'd recognize humanity if it slapped him upside the head.

Which she'd do at the first opportunity.

Because she'd just remembered who else pronounced his *A*s with that same pretentious inflection. Who spoke so precisely, a parody of an educated man. Benton, the workshop instructor.

"So, working for the police, are we?" He dragged her upright and held her bound wrists over her head while he forced her in a two-footed hop to the far side of the warehouse.

"We're onto you, you bastard," she spat through the pain in her head and her torso. "The team is already looking for you." His driver's license photo must be ten years old, and he'd lost some weight. No wonder it had taken her so long to figure it out.

And chances were that if she recognized his voice, then Leah would have, too. And Leah would tell Cooper, who could identify Benton immediately.

"That's difficult to believe, since to my knowledge, we've never met."

"You heard me. I told them where we were."

"Your resourcefulness is admirable, but I'll be finished with you long before they find you. Assuming they do."

Her eyes narrowed in pain and challenge. "I'm a state investigator for the California Law Enforcement Unit. Touch me and you'll go to San Quentin for life."

They had reached the other side of the empty warehouse space, and he pushed her through a door that had once been an office. Now it held a mattress and a scattering of cigarette butts under a window made up of small squares of glass. No one had been here in months.

Joanna's gaze halted on the sill beneath a second window whose panes were all intact. A glint of gold. A pendant shaped like an *S*.

Correction. Danielle had been here. Joanna's gaze dropped to the floor, where a brown stain smeared the concrete.

In the final minutes before Richard Benton had taken her life.

"Casitas! Casitas!"

Cooper and Leah stared at each other, then back at the monitoring deck as though it might somehow sprout a video feed and show them what was happening to Joanna. The next couple of minutes of tape chilled him, and the final burst of static that signaled the demolition of the transmitter sounded as grim as a gunshot.

"So what do we know?" he ground out, trying to sound

normal for Leah's sake. Her olive skin had turned so pale it was nearly gray, and tears glittered in her eyes though she tried to keep her back straight and look like a pro in front of him. "We have a warehouse that's two blocks from something called Casitas. What does that mean?"

Leah gulped. "*Casita* means little house. But I think it's a street name. Lots of the streets here are Spanish words." She ran the audio back a few seconds. "She's finishing her sentence. 'I'm in a warehouse two blocks from Casitas.'"

"Play the rest of it again, from where he says she's awake. Something in there is bugging me."

Her fingers danced over the keyboard and he heard the male voice again.

He knew that voice. The only thing that surprised him was why it had taken him all these minutes to place it.

Because he'd been listening to it for two solid days.

"I know who that is," he said. "It's Richard Benton, the instructor for the Rules of Seduction workshops."

Leah's eyes widened, and she slapped her forehead. "Fire me," she moaned. "Fire me right now. I didn't even pick that up—and it's my job."

Cooper swore, then controlled himself before Leah misunderstood and thought he was angry with her. "Don't beat yourself up. Obviously Joanna didn't recognize his voice, either. Okay. First I get hold of Nate Randall and let him know we've got a suspect in his murder. Then we hit the streets."

He snatched his phone off its charger and dialed Nate's cell. After three rings he wondered if the city cop had turned it off, but then someone answered.

"'Lo?" Uh-oh. The poor guy had probably just fallen asleep.

"Hey. It's Cooper Maxwell. We've got a situation."

"What's up?" The sleepiness cleared out of Nate's tone and a rustling sound in the background told Cooper he'd tossed aside the blankets and sat up.

"Joanna was on the money, Nate. Our guy has a thing for redheads, and now he's abducted her. But I've got a possible ID."

Nate swore. "I'm listening."

"I've been taking these Rules of Seduction workshops, instructed by a guy called Richard Benton. I was listening to Joanna's transmissions until he discovered the wire on her and destroyed it. I recognized his voice. Along with abducting Joanna, there's a high probability he killed Danielle Starkweather."

"Joanna was wearing a wire?"

"Yeah. A wire, but no ear bulb. She did her best to get us a message, but I could use your help figuring out what it means."

"What'd she say?"

"'I'm in a warehouse two blocks from Casitas.' Is that a street? A club? A factory?"

"A street in the warehouse district. We know Danielle wasn't killed where she was found. He's probably got a hidey-hole in one of those buildings."

"Can we get some help canvassing the area? I can't act fast enough with just the three of us. I need beat cops who are familiar with those streets, and I need them within the hour. The half hour. I don't know how much time she has."

"I'll see what I can do."

"No lights, no sirens," Cooper said tersely. "We don't want to tip him off."

"Got it."

Cooper hung up and turned to Leah. "I want everything you can find on Benton," he said. "Pull out all the stops. Family connections, associations, places he likes to hang out. All of it."

"I gave you everything I could get before," Leah said. "There's not a lot out there unless we do it the old-fashioned way down at county records. And they're not open at this time of night."

"Do the best you can." He pulled a transmitter out of her kit and fitted it in his ear. "Wire me up. Then raise Will and brief him on everything. Tell him I'll meet him on Casitas."

While he'd been talking with Nate, she'd brought up a satellite map of Santa Rita. She pointed to an intersection on her monitor. "It's four blocks long. You should meet him here, where it intersects with Ocean, and work from south to north."

"Print that for us, will you?"

She sent the map to their printer and taped him up. When she'd finished, she gripped Cooper's arm. "I'm coming with you."

Her eyes mirrored his own fear. He hoped he wasn't as transparent. He had to lead the troops now, not scare them and make them lose confidence.

"Sorry, Leah. I need you here to be our central point of communications. And I'll need whatever you can get on Benton as soon as you get it."

"There's nothing more I can—"

He took the hand that lay on his arm and gave it a

shake. "This is Joanna we're talking about. Don't let her down."

Famous last words.

He left the safe house at a dead run, his gut churning with dread. Because he'd already done that himself, and he had no way to turn back the clock.

18

227-A San Benito
Santa Rita, California
00:11 hours

THE FACT THAT she was law enforcement didn't seem to faze Richard Benton one bit. In fact, it seemed to give him even more pleasure.

"Then you've no doubt heard what happened to the last of my ladies," he said. "Not much of a constitution, that one. I trust you'll give me more sport."

She'd give him sport, all right.

"Too bad you have to tape your girlfriends down before they'll submit," she snapped. "Or use those stupid Rules to turn them into zombies."

His eyebrows rose. "You've heard of the Rules?"

Mistake.

Her sense of self-preservation kicked in. The less he thought she knew, the better. "Tracey told me."

"Really. And who might that be?"

"You put her in the hospital, you bastard. What is it with you and redheads, anyway?"

His face clouded and his hands flexed and then clenched into fists. "You talk too much. I told you I'd tape your mouth, and I meant it. Don't bother trying to run—this building is secure. Once I've finished with you, you won't be able to anyway. Unless you can swim with your feet like that."

He spun on one heel and his footsteps echoed as he returned to the car. The tape was probably in the trunk. That meant she had a minute, at most, to do something.

Joanna abandoned the futile business of trying to understand the ramblings of a nutcase and zeroed in on the window she'd seen when he'd first pushed her in here. One of the squares of glass was cracked, as though a rock thrown by a truck outside had bounced off it. Cracked meant weakened, and she could work with that.

Awkwardly, she hopped over to it and formed double fists with her hands. This was gonna hurt, but she had no choice and no time to think about it.

With all the controlled force she could muster, she wrapped one fist inside the other and smashed the pane. It shattered with a telltale tinkle and pain screeched up her arms to detonate in her brain. She choked down a sob and sawed the duct tape on a shard sticking up out of the frame.

Only seconds now.

The tape parted, and warm, slippery blood ran down her fingers as she snatched up a shard on the floor and cut the tape holding her ankles together. Blood flowed into them, but not quickly enough.

She was still crouched on the floor, willing her ankles to hold her up, when Richard Benton appeared in the doorway.

"Clever girl," he said. "But it's no good. I'll only tape you up again."

He closed the office door.

"What's the matter?" she taunted, hoping a few seconds of distraction would give her circulation time to bring strength to her feet and ankles. "The Rules don't work? You need tape to subdue your victims?"

"*Victims* is such an ugly word." He measured out a length of thick silver tape and tore it off. "I prefer *lovers*. And no, the Rules don't work."

She blinked. "What?"

"For heaven's sake, girl, surely you don't believe all that mumbo jumbo. Meridians. Energy." He snorted. "Bullshit."

"But they worked on me!" she blurted.

"Did they? How amusing."

While crouching, she tried to bounce on the balls of her feet. Aha. Nearly good to go.

"But you—Tracey said you taught some kind of workshop."

"Did she? I don't remember the girl, so I don't remember the gist of any conversation. But she's right. I teach a workshop. But all it does is give a roomful of saps the spine to actually approach a woman. Most of them don't have the balls or the brains to do it. If handing over fifteen hundred dollars and sitting through ten hours of instruction on how a woman's body actually works makes them more apt to go after what they want, then they've got what they paid for, haven't they?"

"The Rules don't work," she repeated, just to be sure.

"No. I make most of it up. But the physiology and psychology lessons are sound. That's what they need, anyway, the losers."

Then what the hell had happened to her when Thomas Semple had approached her? Never mind. She'd figure that out later.

Benton snapped the length of tape taut between his hands. "Now, is this going to be messy or are you going to be a good girl?"

"Define *good*," she said, and snap-kicked him right in the crotch.

WILL PULLED UP in the unmarked vehicle before Cooper had had a chance to look at his watch more than four times. He bit back an impatient comment and surveyed the eight uniform cops standing on the sidewalk as Will joined them.

"Okay, here's the situation," he said. "Joanna Mac-Pherson has been abducted by Richard Benton, an instructor peddling a series of workshops called the Rules of Seduction. Benton has already abducted two others that we know of—Tracey Bigelow and Danielle Starkweather. Danielle didn't survive—she washed up on the beach in the early hours of Monday morning. Investigator MacPherson was able to get a message to us that she's within two blocks of this street—" he pointed up at the sign "—Casitas, which is four blocks long. You're going to split up into pairs and start at the four corners of the grid on this map, three blocks out from Casitas." Quickly, he handed copies of the satellite map to the men. "Work toward the center. Check every building, every alley, every square foot of your areas."

"Most of these warehouses are locked down," one of the cops objected. "We got warrants for all of them?"

"No. Investigator MacPherson knows we're coming. If she can't make herself visible, she'll make sure she's heard. MacPherson's photograph is on the back of these maps. So is our suspect's, though it's not recent. Stay in constant radio contact, and as you complete each block, radio it in so we can strike that area from the map. Any questions?"

The cops and Will shook their heads.

"Okay. Go."

The tense group scattered, and Will had to jog to keep up with Cooper. "Where are we headed?"

Cooper tapped a spot on the map with one finger as he ran. "I'm starting in the middle and working out."

"Are you gonna let me apologize?" Will panted.

Cooper glanced at him, and slowed to a fast walk. The center point was a block or so away. "For what?"

"For being stupid enough to lose her. I'm responsible for this snafu. If he hurts her, it's my fault."

Jeez, he did not need this now.

"It's not your fault. She was only going to the head, as far as you knew."

"Yeah, but I was covering her. I should have gone, too."

"And she'd have chewed your ear off all the way to the bar."

"You'll take my resignation, right?" Will's tone held determination and the kind of firmness that covered up fear. "As soon as this is over."

Cooper stopped in the gutter. There were no sidewalks in this part of town because nobody walked anywhere anymore. A yard light caught the glitter of Will's eyes. And the pain.

"Don't be an idiot. I need you focused on finding

Joanna, not beating yourself up over what you can't change. She won't thank you for it. Got that?"

Will took a deep breath, and swallowed whatever else he had been about to say. "Yes, sir."

"Good. Now, pay attention. Starting from here, we're working outward. Take that side of the street. Keep your mouth shut and your ears open."

"Yes, sir."

This part of town would never win a beauty contest on its best day, but tonight every foot of it seemed to hold danger. Broken glass, tin cans and bits of abandoned machinery lay in pockets of darkness, waiting to trip and injure. Cooper trained the high-intensity halogen flashlight he'd borrowed from the P.D. on the ground and up the sides of the buildings, forcing himself to listen when he wanted to shout her name over and over like a madman until she heard him.

Until she knew help was on the way.

Hang on, Joanna. Don't let him win.

He peered into darkened windows, running the white beam of light over everything from auto bodies to stored sailboats to pallets of what looked like rice. And while his brain catalogued what his eyes observed, his heart thundered in his chest with pent-up adrenaline and fear for her safety.

Had there ever been a bigger fool in the history of CLEU? Probably not. It had been staring him in the face for days now, and he'd chosen to downgrade it, to make it less than the wonder that it was, and for what?

Pride? His own way?

Idiot.

Picking his way through the dark, he tried doors,

rattled locks and got up close and personal with corrugated metal, concrete and chain-link fencing. Now, there was a visual metaphor for you. He had emotional chain link all around his heart. He'd been so proud of himself for his skill at forming teams, so cool about the brotherhood of law enforcement personified by himself, Kellan, Danny and Jim, that he'd completely missed the significance of Joanna's impact on his life.

Well, he wasn't missing it now. He'd run up against the kind of fear he'd never experienced before. Not the personal kind. He'd faced an armed drug dealer on a dock and not felt anything except a businesslike determination to bag his guy and go home. No, this was fear for someone else, and it shook him.

Because of what it meant.

Fear this deep meant you cared this deep.

Doesn't it, buddy? You care. You care so much it scares you. And unless you get your butt in gear and find her, she'll never know it.

He had no idea how she felt. Right now she probably hated his guts for not supporting her all-too-correct hunch about Richard Benton. He hadn't supported her, and it resulted in her taking an inexperienced cover man. Logic told him that she was a seasoned investigator who had to have known what she was getting into, but logic didn't have any effect on the way he felt.

This was the woman he wanted, and how she'd fallen into danger didn't matter. What mattered was getting her out of it before the worst happened.

His mind shut down and wouldn't let him go any further. If he thought about what Benton had done to

Danielle Starkweather, he'd go insane and start pulling down rusty corrugated walls with his bare hands.

"Vista Base to Cooper," Leah's voice said in his ear.

"Go, Base," he replied quietly. He, Will and the Santa Rita team were all on a dedicated channel, with no routine traffic allowed. With a fellow officer in mortal danger, all jurisdictional bets were off. Nate Randall had come through like a champ.

"I have some more information," Leah said. "I ran Benton through the police and military databases and got a hit. He was in the marines for about six months. Medical discharge."

"Why?"

"Unstable mental condition. No further information."

"Good work."

"There's more."

He and Will had reached the corner of their block. He motioned for Will to go one way, and he turned left and took the other. "Go."

"I discovered that county records are all online here. We don't know where his actual base is, but Benton owns property in the unincorporated area north of Santa Rita, left to him by his mother"

"Nate, get out there. He may have thrown us off the track and gone to ground where he knows the terrain."

"Ten-four," Nate's voice said. "On our way."

"Motor Vehicles had Mrs. Benton's photograph on file," Leah went on. "A little creepy, if you ask me. She's got red hair."

It was tempting to build a profile and conclude that Benton had issues with his mother that had compelled him to murder. But Cooper's training told him it had to be more complicated than that. "Any info on her cause of death?"

"Santa Rita P.D. had a report. According to the death certificate, it was a broken neck due to a fall."

Nate's voice broke in. "How long ago was this?"

"The death certificate is dated 1992."

"Thanks, Leah," Cooper said. "Nice job."

"It's Joanna, like you said," she said simply. "Base out."

Cooper turned left again and began to make his way down the alley that ran parallel to the street he'd just canvassed. Will reported that he'd reached his corner and was doing the same down the alley on the other side of the street. The beat cops checked in one by one, and he pictured Leah ghosting out section after section of the master map on her screen.

At least they had an explanation for the systematic violence perpetrated on Danielle's body. The information they had to date pointed to the possibility that Benton's violence had escalated from assault to rape to murder. He could be a serial killer and they just hadn't found the other bodies yet. Or, something may have triggered him in the last months, setting him off on a rising rampage. And if his pattern held true and he escalated his capture of Joanna to some previously untried level of violence...

Cooper felt the adrenaline spike in his gut and he quickened his steps down the alley, picking his path between cardboard boxes, refuse and barrels.

A second later he heard a sound—and it hadn't come from the transmitter in his ear, either.

A seagull? Not at this time of night.

A rat? No.

Where had it come from?

Come on. Come on, whoever you are. Make another noise.

A pathway clogged with garbage ran off to his right. Training his flashlight beam on the ground so he wouldn't puncture his feet with a forgotten spike or gaff hook, he moved cautiously between two warehouse buildings. The one on his right was corrugated metal, but the one on the left was solid concrete. Had the sound come from the metal building with its thinner walls?

"Son of a bitch!" he heard faintly. And there was the sound again—the chirp of spinning tires.

He knew that voice. Adrenaline flooded his system, putting every sense on alert. High on one side of the concrete building was an open window. He'd swear in court the voice had come through it.

"Team!" he said, breaking into a run. "I think I've got her. San Benito, on the back side of Casitas. Concrete building. I'll confirm the address in a second."

He dashed around the corner, scattering a heap of trash cans with a crash. From behind the roll-up door with the letter *A* stenciled on it in yellow, he heard the roar of a car engine and the shriek of tires.

The roll-up door rose a few feet, and a cloud of exhaust puffed out from under it. Before it had opened more than six feet or so, a late-model BMW screamed out of the opening, its engine revved so high the tach was probably buried in the red zone.

Naked to the waist, eyes wild and swearing like a sailor on shore leave, Joanna MacPherson spun the wheel and fishtailed onto the street.

19

227-A San Benito
Santa Rita, California
00:34 hours

A MAN'S BODY flung itself at the window and Joanna screamed, instinctively covering her face with one arm as she spun the wheel with the other hand, trying to dislodge him. How had Benton escaped so fast? Dammit! Had he pulled the same trick she had with the broken glass and the tape? She could swear he'd been out cold when she'd dashed from that ugly office and stolen his car.

"Joanna!" someone shouted, but it was nothing more than background noise to her panic.

She swerved again and he fell away, releasing her to blessed, blessed freedom. She tromped on the gas and the BMW streaked down the nearest street. She didn't know where she was or what it was called, but she didn't care, either.

All she cared about was putting as much distance as possible between herself and Richard Benton.

Oh yeah, and telling the team where she was. And where they could find him. She had to do that, too—as soon as she could guarantee he wasn't after her. As soon as she felt safe.

Two men stepped into the road fifty feet in front of her.

Benton! No!

Wait. Uniform cops. Safety.

She jammed both feet on the antilock brakes and slid to a controlled stop between them.

"Investigator MacPherson?" one of them asked through the closed window. "Ma'am? My God, are you all right?"

I am now. She found the right button and lowered the window. "He's in the warehouse," she choked out, her heart thumping in overdrive and her hands shaking from the adrenaline rush. "Suspect is Benton—Richard Benton. I left him back there. Taped to his own goddamn desk."

The other cop spoke into the radio at his shoulder. "We've got her," he said. "She's safe. Intersection of Ninth and Pacific. She advises suspect Benton is still in the building, taped to a table."

While the second cop ran the plate on the BMW, the first one opened the door and helped her out of the driver's seat. He took off his jacket and wrapped it around her, and the warmth it held made her realize how deathly cold she was.

That bastard Benton had not only ripped her blouse off, he'd managed to get her bra, too, during the few seconds between recovering from her blow to his balls and the final KO she'd delivered with her cut hands to the back of his skull.

Footsteps pounded up behind them and she flinched, dropping to a crouch and getting ready to take him on a third time.

Cooper Maxwell knelt beside her, panting, struggling for control. Then he gave it up and grabbed her, pulling her against his chest.

"Joanna," he murmured. "It's over. Thank God. I knew you'd hang on. I knew it."

She collapsed sideways and wrapped both arms tightly around his waist, burrowing into his warmth, his concern and his sheer saneness. He knelt on the cold asphalt of the road and pulled her into his lap, stroking her hair and murmuring things that didn't make a lot of sense.

But she didn't care.

Nothing mattered but being in his arms. Having him between her and the specter of Richard Benton. She inhaled the scent of Cooper's sweat and fear for her, mixed with the last lingering traces of some cologne he'd put on this morning.

Morning seemed very far away. But as long as there was safety in the night, she'd take it and be grateful.

"Sir?" One of the officers was trying to get Cooper's attention.

He sighed, as if resigning himself to the fact that he couldn't just scoop her up and disappear with her. They still had work to do. "Yeah? Is he in custody?"

Slowly, he helped Joanna to her feet. Her knees wobbled, and she straightened them, willing herself to stand. She pulled the cop's jacket closer around her and began to snap the fastenings up the front.

"That's the problem, sir. We need to confirm the warehouse. There doesn't seem to be anyone in the one you and Investigator MacPherson indicated, sir."

"What?" Cooper stared at the cop in complete incomprehension.

Joanna stopped doing up snaps. "I'll show you." Thank God her voice sounded strong, even though the rest of her trembled like an aspen leaf in a strong wind. "We can see it from here." Had she really only driven half a block? It seemed like miles. She pointed. "That one, with the open roll-up door. Your guys are all over it."

"Yes, ma'am. But there's no one inside."

"Impossible." Strength surged into her legs as she took off in the direction of the door. "I left him in an office in the back, taped to a desk."

Flanked by the two uniforms and Cooper, she found the guts to walk back to her prison and cross the echoing space inside the warehouse. When they reached the office in the rear, Will looked up. His face changed.

Will, if you cry, so help me, I'll never forgive you.

He didn't, but the pain and guilt in his eyes almost made her do so. "Thank God you're all right," he said simply. "How did you get away?"

She held up her hands and gestured at the broken window. "I cut myself free. I think he's had some combat training, but I don't think he was expecting mine." Cooper swore under his breath.

"The ambulance is here," one of the cops told them. "Somebody should look at those cuts."

Joanna had seen it, waiting nearby, but they couldn't hang around so that the EMTs could doctor her. "I don't know how he got away—I used half a roll taping him down. But it doesn't matter. We need to quit standing around and go after him."

"Nate Randall is already on it," Cooper said. "Benton owns property outside the city limits. Ten to one he'll go there."

"How's he going to do that?" Joanna objected. "I stole his car."

Will grinned. "His only choice is a bus."

But Cooper wasn't in the mood for jokes, if his set jaw and pale skin were any indication. "He's still around here somewhere, hiding out and waiting for us to leave. How bad did you hurt him?" He looked into Joanna's face.

"I kicked him in the balls and dropped him with two fists to the back of his neck," she said succinctly, and one of the uniforms gulped and moved away an inch or two. "He'll be sore but not incapacitated."

"We need to bring in some more bodies," Cooper said to the uniforms. "Walk our grids again and flush him out."

"What if he took off?" Will wanted to know. "He can't be hurt that bad if he woke up, freed himself and ran in less than ten minutes. What if he walked downtown to cruise the clubs? He could pick up a woman with a ride and be miles away by now."

A fragment, a few words, flashed into Joanna's memory. "He didn't."

They looked up as a car pulled up outside and Nate Randall and another plainclothes detective got out. They jogged over, and even though its snaps were fastened, Joanna pulled the jacket even more tightly around herself.

Had no one heard her? It had only been a few words, but the possibility was huge. She needed to make them underst—

"I thought you were checking Benton's property," Cooper said.

"I have a team staked out on the road and at the residence there," Nate said. "This is my crime scene. I'm waiting for the forensics team to get here to process it."

"But I'm okay," Joanna said. "He didn't get much further than assault."

"Not yours." His tone was terse. "Danielle's."

"Guys, we're wasting time," Will said from the back of the group. "Need a plan, here."

"If his property's covered, then we'll work the downtown area," Cooper told them. "I'll take Will and these officers. Joanna, you're going with the EMTs to the hospital. I'm not taking any chances."

"No," she said.

"Good." He turned to the officers and pulled the satellite map out of his pocket. "Now—"

"He didn't go downtown."

Cooper stopped in midword and stared at her. So did the uniforms. "What?"

"He said something. When he dragged me in here. Something about hoping I could swim with my feet like that. You know, taped together."

"So?" Cooper's eyebrows dipped in a frown. "Sounds like a reference to Danielle."

"Sure it was. Think about it. How did she get into the water? Did he roll her off a pier? He must have a boat tied up somewhere."

"A boat." Cooper looked as though he wanted to check her forehead for fever. She couldn't see why.

"Cooper, the guy is a coward. He's on the run. He won't troll the clubs for a woman and waste time chatting someone up when he's desperate for transportation." She thought he might interrupt her, but he didn't. He just looked at her with that long gaze. "Danielle got into the water somehow, and it's a lot easier to pretend your girl had too much to drink and get her onto your boat than it is to walk five hundred feet out onto a pier with a body over your shoulder."

"Leah?" Cooper said.

Everyone except Joanna had a transmitter bulb.

"She's already on it," the cop who had given Joanna his jacket relayed the transmission. "No marine vessels of any kind are registered to Richard Benton."

"But he—."

"Good theory," Cooper told Joanna. "But let's stick to probabilities. If he's on foot, the highest probability is that he'll steal or hijack a vehicle at the earliest opportunity. Get downtown. Alert everyone on patrol to watch for erratic drivers. He may be forcing someone to take him to a bigger town where he can confuse the trail."

No. This wasn't right. "Cooper, you need to listen to me. Maybe the boat's registered under a different name. Maybe—"

But the man who had been so closely attuned to every nuance of her body only a few nights ago, who had stroked sensation from her skin as though it were music, was in full alpha command mode now.

Which meant he wasn't listening. To anything. Including nuance, hunch, or anything else that wasn't as certain as that BMW out there.

"Come on," he said to her in a slightly gentler tone. "We'll get you looked after."

Fine. She'd give in on this one and then try to circle back. With any luck, he'd leave her with the EMTs and go chase his probabilities, leaving her free to do the same. And then they'd see who brought home the results.

When the EMTs tried to get the jacket off her so they

could tend to her hands and arms, everything came to a temporary halt. Cooper recovered first.

"Here." He pulled off his shirt and she saw he had a gray T-shirt on underneath. "Put this on."

Uh, where? They stood in the middle of the street, surrounded by the red-and-blue flashing lights. The forensic team had arrived while they were strategizing, and two men and a woman were unloading their kits from a van. There was no way she was getting into the back of the ambulance. Once she conceded that much, they could slam the doors on her and whisk her off to the hospital—and she'd never get a chance to prove she was right.

She took the shirt and walked around the side of the ambulance, shrugging out of the jacket with her naked back turned to the circus. Cooper stepped behind her and picked the jacket off the ground, using it the way her mother had used a beach towel long ago, when they'd changed out of their wet swimsuits before they got into the car.

"Thanks," she said, buttoning his shirt up over her breasts as though she stripped in public all the time. "You didn't have to do that." She rolled the cuffs up over her wrists.

"Yes, I did," he said. "You're not on display. You've been through a massive trauma. And—" He stopped.

"And?"

She could see words bottled up behind his teeth, words that he clearly didn't want to say in front of fifty witnesses. Then he seemed to come to a decision.

"And we're a team," he said with difficulty.

That wasn't what he'd meant to say, she was sure of it. But there wasn't time to press him.

And if the truth be told, all she wanted was to press her cheek against his chest and feel his arms around her once more. To lose herself in that comfort and never come out again. To forget that tonight had ever happened and go back to what they had been on the sailboat.

But she couldn't. She had to deceive him one more time to prove that she was right.

Because that's what it's all about, isn't it?

She watched him walk away and held out her hands to the EMT. The sting of the antiseptic was as painful as the truth.

As much as she wanted to let all this go and do as he asked, she couldn't. Because then she'd be just another woman to be protected from prying eyes, protected from injury, protected from…herself. When he looked at her, she wanted him to see a capable fellow officer of the law, not one more helpless female that had to be hustled offstage before she hurt herself.

You're in the way now, she'd heard her father say countless times in her memory. *Go help your mother, you can't help me here.*

If she didn't do something, nothing would change.

Well, things would be different tonight. She'd track Richard Benton down herself if she had to. She'd bring him back in cuffs and they'd all see that she was an investigator to be reckoned with. Hadn't she saved herself from him the first time? Huh? No white knight had to come riding in to save her. She could do it on her own.

She wouldn't waste Cooper Maxwell's time or that

of his team of uniforms. She had unfinished business with Richard Benton.

She'd taken care of business alone before. And she could damn well do it again.

20

TALK ABOUT A needle in a haystack.

Cooper and his team had canvassed every bar and club in a four-block square—which was pretty much all of the downtown area. The Santa Rita guys had distributed Richard Benton's photograph from the DMV database, and after what felt like several hundred women had shaken their heads and looked blank, Cooper's frustration levels had hit an all-time high.

To say that time was running out was the understatement of the year. If they didn't catch Benton tonight, he'd go underground and then pop up in some other community, free to peddle his workshops and take his time looking for another victim, and another department would have a homicide on their hands.

"Vista Base to team," Leah said in his ear.

"Go, Base." He glanced at Will and they stepped outside Atlantis onto the street, where they could hear her. Up at the corner, he could see a uniform showing the photograph to a busker with a guitar on the sidewalk. The guy was shaking his head.

How many officers were pulling a double shift tonight?

"I've been running some queries," Leah said, an uncharacteristic diffidence in her tone. "I heard Joanna mention that maybe the sailboat might be registered in someone else's name."

Cooper sighed. "Leah, there is no sailboat. We need you focused on assisting us, not—"

"I'm sorry, sir, but I got a hit."

Any urge to remind her of her duty died in midthought. "Go."

"Benton doesn't have a sailboat, but there are more people in this case than him, right? So I started running names. Thomas Semple. Julian Royden. Afrodita Enterprises. Anth—"

"Leah," Cooper said patiently. "The bottom line, okay?"

"I was just getting there. Anthony Bingham, one of the directors of Afrodita Enterprises, has a sailboat, the *Snow Queen*. A fifty-four-foot Hunter, registered in Long Beach and bearing number KAZ2-Y5KS."

"Joanna was right," Will said, glaring at him.

"Not necessarily," Cooper snapped. What did he have to glare about? Joanna was no more than a teammate to him. "That's a pretty thin connection. It's probably in Long Beach. Or Seattle. Or Cabo San Lucas."

"We still have to check it out." Will held Cooper's gaze, making it personal even though every word they said was being broadcast citywide over two agencies. "And if you don't, I will." Every line of his surfer's body held challenge.

Cooper had the authority to smack him with an insubordination report, but something in his gut told him to give the kid a chance.

Because they all knew they couldn't afford any loose ends.

"Everyone on Pacific, report to me in front of Atlantis," he barked. "We're stretched, but somebody has to check out the harbor. Everyone deployed on other streets, keep up your canvassing. We'll do as we did before. Report in at the end of every block. Will, come with me."

Four uniforms materialized out of the dark, and he and Will jumped into their vehicles with two each for company. No lights, no sirens, even though the un-marked vehicles were equipped with both. They'd go in quietly and hope they weren't too late.

At least he could be thankful for one thing. By now Joanna would've been transported to the hospital. She'd be safe and out of harm's way.

You should have told her.

Told her what? That he cared? With lights flashing and radios squawking and cops swarming everywhere, it hadn't been the right time or place to say what he wanted to say. It needed to be somewhere quiet, away from re-minders of what they both did for a living. He, at least, needed that. If you were going to love someone, they were like a refuge for you. A place you could go to—

Wait a minute. What did you just say?

His foot jerked on the gas pedal and the speedome-ter needle crept upward another tick.

When exactly had *that* happened?

But he already knew.

The moment when he'd seen her standing in the street, some cop's jacket around her, and she'd gone into his arms as if that was the only place on the planet she wanted to be. He'd known with a cutting clarity he'd never experienced before that this was his woman, that her courage and toughness and yes, recklessness, were a match for his own. That they could take on life side by side, and woe to anyone who got in their way.

She was his match. His partner. His lover.

The woman he respected and needed.

The woman he loved.

That knowledge created a core of warmth inside him. He'd wrap this job and then go to her. He wasn't a hundred percent sure how she felt, or whether she would ever be able to see past the trauma to the future. So anything beyond that would be up to her.

He could wait.

They crossed the railroad tracks and dove down the slope toward the harbor. From here he could see the tangled forest of masts that gave them the location of the recreational marina, as opposed to the section of the harbor that housed commercial fishing boats.

Both cars crunched to a halt in the empty parking lot and Cooper surveyed the situation quickly as he got out of the car. "There are five quays," he said tersely. "Every man take a quay. When you find the *Snow Queen,* don't approach. Let us know the location and we'll surround it. Will, you come with me."

The marina was surrounded with chain-link fencing, but the door in the center wasn't locked. That in itself was a little strange, but Cooper didn't stop to think about it. He and Will loped quietly down the center quay, trying for as much stealth as possible on the plank decking.

Mermaid, Gonzo Fishin', Mary Ellis.

No *Snow Queen.* Had Leah made an error? Or worse, was Bingham's boat moored at some other marina that they weren't familiar with?

"Any luck?" he breathed into the transmitter.

The harbor team checked in one by one, all negative.

"How many marinas are in the area?"

"This is it until Monterey," one of the cops said. "There was another one on the south side of town, but it silted up. Too shallow for boats this size."

Hole in the Water.

Diana.

Snow—He sucked in a breath. *Snowbird.* Shit.

"Keep looking," he said.

Barmy, Retirement Dream, Elizabeth Swann.

He was almost at the end of the quay, with half a dozen boats to go.

"Cooper." Will grabbed him by the arm. "There she is."

"*Snow Queen?* Where?"

Fifty-four feet long. That knocked out this one and the next one. How could Will see the names on these damn things when he—

"Not the boat," Will said. He sounded strange. Choked. Cooper stared at him.

Will pulled him down behind a small white vessel that bobbed at its moorings. He pointed at the second-to-last boat on the right.

"I meant Joanna."

JOANNA COULD HEAR Richard Benton rummaging around down in the cabin of the boat. She knelt on the deck of the vessel tied up next to his, concealed behind the mast, and considered her options while she breathed deeply and tried to keep the adrenaline levels down.

It hadn't been easy getting away from the EMTs, who had been as determined to get her to the hospital as she was to evade them. They had wheels. But she had the dark, and she knew where she was going.

She'd taken off on foot and lost them within a block.

Benton hadn't had much of a start, and with her police conditioning coupled with regular workouts, she caught up with him within a couple of blocks. He maintained a laboring but dogged pace over the half mile between the warehouse and the marina, one she was able to match easily while she kept out of sight.

When she'd followed him to the boat, she had the advantage of a nice prearrest warm-up, while he'd been exhausted. As soon as he came topside again, she'd leap to the deck and make the arrest, with the help of the handcuffs she'd lifted from the nice cop who'd lent her his jacket. She wished she had a service weapon, too, but that would have been harder to steal. She'd make do with what she had—her feet. She'd overpowered Benton once. She could do it again.

The boat tilted in the water and she whirled to see two dark shapes climbing onboard. Did Benton have accomplices? A scream was out of the question. She tensed and crouched, ready to spring like a wildcat in her own defense.

"Joanna!"

The taller one whispered her name a second before she recognized the shaggy mane of Will Stutz on the shorter man.

Cooper.

He'd believed her. She wasn't quite sure how he'd gotten there—after having discounted her theory in front of everyone—but she wouldn't argue about it now. He was here, and she had backup. Armed backup.

Her prospects alone had been neutral at best. Now she knew Richard Benton didn't stand a chance.

"Situation report."

Clearly he wasn't about to waste time yelling at her for not going to the hospital, though she was damn sure he'd probably have plenty to say after this was over. But for now, they were in this together and it looked as though he'd play it straight ahead.

"He's in the cabin of his boat," she said rapidly, pointing. "He'll be out any second to cast off."

"It's not his," Will told her in as low a tone. "It belongs to one of the Afrodita Enterprises directors, Anthony Bingham. Registered in Long Beach."

Like a marionette, she turned her head to stare at him. "Anthony Bingham owns it?"

Cooper nodded. "It's called the *Snow Queen*."

Joanna fought back the urge to laugh. "Either he's got a sick sense of humor, or he's too cocky for his own good. Bingham's one of L.A.'s biggest coke distributors."

"Also known as 'snow,'" Will breathed. "Very funny."

"We've never been able to pin anything on him," Joanna told them, one eye on its still empty decks. "Which is why it felt good to nail daddy's boy for pimping. I wonder why he keeps his boat moored here?"

"Maybe he owes Benton something?" Cooper asked. "Loans it to him as a favor?"

"Shhh." Will touched both their arms as Richard Benton emerged onto the deck.

They could hear the rasp of his breathing as he moved around the deck, releasing the canvas and getting the boat ready to move.

"Plan?" Will asked, looking from Cooper to Joanna.

"I'm going to jump over there when he's busy unwrapping the ropes from the cleat on the far side," Joanna said. "He won't see me until it's too late."

"He'll hear you," Cooper said. "It's too dangerous. Will and I will board while you distract him from the dock."

"I'm taking him." Joanna spoke fiercely, as Benton moved to a cleat in the stern and began the casting-off process. "After what he did to me, it's my right."

"You've been injured enough tonight," Cooper said. "I need to keep you safe."

"It's not about what you need!"

"Guys," Will said, peering over the wheelhousing, "he's done three ropes. We're out of time."

"Joanna," Cooper said softly. "Trust me."

Her plan had been a good one—if she'd been alone. But she wasn't alone. She was no longer a cowboy, striking out furiously on her own the way she'd done when she'd taken down "Bling" Bingham and nearly killed him. She was Cooper's partner, and though they'd both lost sight of that, he was giving her the chance to regain it.

She nodded once, and as Richard Benton moved to release the final rope tethering the *Snow Queen* to its moorage, she leaped lightly down from the stern and strolled down the dock to where he stood at the rail.

"Going somewhere?" she asked pleasantly.

He jerked and dropped the thick rope, then recovered himself.

"You're like a bad penny," he said.

She counted four coils around the cleat. *Come on, Cooper, make your move.*

"Not exactly good luck for you," she agreed. "Richard Benton, I'm placing you under arrest for so many crimes I can't begin to list them, but we'll start with the first-degree murder of Danielle Starkweather and assaulting a peace officer with the intent to cause grave bodily harm."

"You won't be doing much arresting from down there." He unwrapped a coil of rope. Then another. "Unless you plan to join me and continue our sport?"

Cooper—

Out of the corner of her eye, she saw Will and Cooper leap from one deck to the other like a pair of pirates.

Third coil.

They landed on the deck on either side of him, each about six feet away, cutting off his access to the cabin on one side and his escape down the deck on the other.

"Drop that rope, Benton," Cooper ordered. "Step away from the rail and put your hands on the back of your head."

Slowly, Benton dropped the rope. Joanna moved down the dock to form the third point of the triangle, cutting off the land route as well. Through the forest of masts on the landward side, she saw the sparkle of blue-and-red flashing lights. The cavalry, having no doubt heard the entire exchange over the transmitters, was on its way at full gallop.

Richard Benton had no choice but to—

Jump—

He landed neatly next to her and grabbed her around the neck, pushing her in front of him to make a human shield.

Oh, shit, Joanna, not again—

She drew her elbow back to let him have it in the ribs, and he grabbed it and twisted it up between their bodies. In the other hand he held the thickest, nastiest-looking knife she'd ever seen.

Suddenly she understood how he'd escaped from her tape job so fast. She'd searched his bloody pockets but he'd obviously had it in some kind of leg holster. He laid it against her jugular.

She cried out, and Will leaped to the rail as if he were about to jump down. "Let her go. You can't win. You're surrounded."

"Not likely," Benton said. "Get off the boat. Now. Once I'm onboard and moving, you can have her."

The dock area seemed to be swarming with uniformed cops, but not one of them would be any help if she couldn't get herself free.

Slowly, deliberately, Cooper and Will walked down the gangplank.

"Back twenty feet," Benton said.

At the far end of the dock, the cavalry began pounding toward them.

Cooper and Will moved back, and pain lanced through Joanna's arm and shoulders as Benton duck-walked her up the gangplank onto the deck. He bent her over at the waist. "Untie that rope."

They were at an impasse, and with only seconds in which to make a decision, Joanna did the only thing she could—she took herself out of the equation. Without halting her forward momentum, she lifted her feet off the deck.

Off balance, Richard Benton tilted forward under the sudden burden of a hundred and thirty unexpected pounds. She rolled toward him to take the pressure off her arm and then with a single kick off the deck, launched herself into the narrow ribbon of water between the hull and the timbers of the dock.

As she hit the water and went under, she heard a reverberating boom that could only mean one thing.

Somebody had fired his service weapon, and the paperwork was going to be a bitch.

21

THE DISCIPLINARY TRIBUNAL had been scheduled for ten o'clock, and now it was pushing eleven-thirty and Joanna still didn't know if she had a career left to go back to after lunch.

It had been eight days since her unexpected swim in the Santa Rita harbor, seven since her return to Los Angeles, five since she'd been placed on administrative leave and four since she'd been informed that her involvement in the police shooting of Richard Benton was to be formally examined.

And in all that time, she hadn't heard one word from Cooper Maxwell.

You'd think that after everything they'd been through, he'd at least have called to say "thanks for the memories." Or sent an e-mail. Or sent up a flare in farewell as her flight passed over downtown San Francisco.

But no. Guy-like, he'd disappeared with as much finality—and with as much notice—as the late unlamented Michael Dunn. What was it with her and goodbyes? Could men not bring themselves to say the words to her? Or did they, as Carleen had told her, think she'd overreact and break something?

She hadn't pegged Cooper for a coward. But hey, she'd obviously had him pegged wrong from the beginning. She'd actually thought there might be something worth fighting for between them—something they ought to give a chance, to see where it would go. But maybe she just didn't have the gift when it came to relationships. Maybe she was meant to go through life alone.

Now, there was a cheery thought on a completely depressing day. She slid down a little in her chair, which she was sure they'd given her because it was so uncomfortable.

Since ten o'clock, they'd been through her mistakes in exhaustive detail, starting with "Bling" Bingham and winding up with her in the Santa Rita harbor while Will Stutz took down Richard Benton from twenty feet away.

He'd thought Benton had stabbed her.

She'd thought her move was an evasive tactic.

It wasn't clear what Benton thought, since he was in the Santa Rita morgue waiting for someone—anyone— to come and claim his remains.

In any event, somehow Will's firing his service weapon had become her fault, too, and here she was, with maybe forty minutes left to go in the career she loved. Carleen had once told her that people often took up second careers after they hit their thirties. Joanna couldn't imagine it. Police work was what she loved— what she was good at. If she didn't have that, what would she do? What would become of her?

Sitting at the defendant's table, she shuddered. The three members of the tribunal sat across from her at their own table, in front of the crossed flags of the United States and California.

"The tribunal calls Investigator Cooper Maxwell of the San Francisco Sub-Unit," said the CO of Internal Affairs. The door opened and Cooper walked in.

Oh, man, he cleans up nice, was her first thought.

Oh, God, he knows too much, was her second.

Would he tell them that he had made love to her on the trunk of a 2005 Ford sedan? Would he say that from the very beginning of his acquaintance with her, her temper had been uncertain and her investigative methods unsound? Would he—

Her thoughts jangled to a stop as he seated himself at the table next to her and they faced Jorge Ramirez, her unit CO; Martina Corelli, the Internal Affairs officer; and James Wilson, the head of C.I.D., the criminal investigations division for the entire state. And the questions began—the same ones they'd asked of her partner at the time of the Bingham debacle, who hadn't actually been there, and of Isabella Waring, her NCO, who at least had heard Joanna's side of it. Then they got specific.

"Please state the nature of your working relationship with Investigator MacPherson," Wilson said to Cooper. The pad in front of him was covered in notes. Joanna wondered if his decision was already made, and he was merely writing stuff down for entertainment's sake. The proceedings were, after all, being digitally taped.

"My relationship with her is based on the utmost respect and regard for her skills as an investigator,"

Cooper said quietly. Joanna resisted the urge to turn and gawk at him. What kind of politically correct corporate-speak was this?

"I find that she adapts her working style to the situation," Cooper went on. "For example, the Benton investigation called for us to think on our feet and make decisions on the fly. The stakes escalated every time we went out on the street. Investigator MacPherson was able to adapt to each of those changing circumstances in a manner that enabled us to get the information we needed while still preserving our cover."

"Can you be specific?" Ramirez asked. He was the only one on this panel she actually knew. The others existed in some kind of executive Olympus up in Sacramento, the state capitol. She'd just as soon they'd stayed there, thanks. They were meant to impart objectivity to the proceedings, but the final effect was that she didn't feel she had a single ally to whom she could state her case.

With the possible exception of Cooper Maxwell.

It was clear he had something unexpected up his beautifully tailored sleeve, but at the moment she wasn't sure she wanted to know what it was.

"Certainly, sir." Cooper took a breath and consulted his notes. "A good example was when we apprehended one Julian Royden. He was a student of these Rules of Seduction we'd been investigating, and it was clear that he intended to assault Investigator MacPherson, whom he'd just picked up at a club. At the time we didn't know if he would become violent, but MacPherson was prepared. She was able to apprehend Royden and her subsequent interview with him netted us some vital information."

Martina Corelli looked up from her pristine notepad. "Did her apprehension of Royden involve violence?"

"She took him to the ground, I believe," Cooper said.

"Was he injured in any way?"

"Shouldn't we be talking about my injuries?" Joanna blurted.

She'd never realized before how impassive a pair of brown eyes could be. Corelli leveled her with a glance. "Investigator MacPherson, please remain silent while we conduct our investigation. But to answer your question, it's your history of violence toward perpetrators we're most concerned with in this hearing."

Great. Poor little perps, with their short sentences and expensive cars. Big mean Joanna, with her short career and expensive condo payment. The corners of her lips turned down and she subsided once again into the uncomfortable chair.

"Let's turn now to the night of the shooting," Wilson said. "I understand from the testimony of Investigator Stutz and from the surveillance tapes maintained by Investigator Martinez that MacPherson disobeyed a direct order to proceed to the hospital for treatment of her injuries and pursued Richard Benton on foot, unassisted." He looked over his glasses at Joanna. "Is that correct?"

"I—well—" Joanna gulped. "Yes. Technically."

"And that you informed no one of your intention to pursue?"

"She informed me," Cooper said.

Wilson glanced at his notes. "She informed you before you instructed her to go to the hospital. You discounted her reasons for a pursuit and proceeded to downtown Santa Rita with your street team."

"Yes. But when we got new information—which you heard on the tapes—from Investigator Martinez, whom I've recommended for a commendation, by the way, I realized Jo— MacPherson was correct in her prediction of Benton's action. I then pursued her to the harbor, where we joined forces again."

"And how long had she maintained her pursuit alone?"

"It couldn't have been more than fifteen minutes. She was, as you noted, on foot. We had a vehicle. We caught up to her before she had time to do more than survey the situation."

He made her sound so organized, so professional. Joanna eyed him sideways. What was going on here? He had nothing to lose by feeding her to the wolves and making himself look good. Instead, he was presenting the whole fiasco as though her run to the harbor had been a mere detour before the team met up again to set some big plan in motion.

She hadn't had a plan. She'd been running on instinct and sheer bullheaded determination not to let Benton get away, and to hell with what anybody else was doing.

But she couldn't very well say *that,* now, could she?

"You've heard Investigator Stutz's reasons for discharging his weapon," Cooper went on. "All I will say was that, from where we stood, it did appear as if Benton had stabbed MacPherson. In my opinion as senior investigator, Stutz's reaction was in keeping with CLEU procedure when an officer goes down."

"Putting him in that position is not in keeping with CLEU procedure," Ramirez observed.

"That's true, but I want to counter that," Martina Corelli said unexpectedly. "If you think about this from a woman's point of view, what MacPherson did was reasonable. Benton outweighed her, and he was armed. She used her body to put him off balance and free herself. All of us are taught that move in self-defense class at the academy. I'm surprised Investigator Stutz didn't recognize it."

"It was dark," Joanna said helpfully. "All of us were blasting adrenaline and everything happened so fast he probably just saw the knife and then me falling, did the math, and acted."

"Thank you for that assessment, Investigator Mac-Pherson," Corelli said. If Joanna had thought she might find an ally in this woman, she was going to have to think again.

"I'd like to add new information to what happened afterward," Cooper said.

"Go ahead," Wilson replied. "After MacPherson was—finally—transported to hospital?"

"Yes." He glanced at Joanna and she wondered what was coming. Was the other shoe about to drop? Should she seriously consider practicing "Do you want fries with that?" in front of the mirror when she got home?

"For the past several days I've been involved in a case that will probably have ramifications up and down the west coast for the rest of this year," he said. Corelli and Ramirez glanced at each other, and Wilson, head of C.I.D., smiled like a cat who has slurped the last of the cream. Cooper glanced at Joanna again. "When we found MacPherson at the dock, we informed her of the name of Bingham's sailboat, which is the *Snow Queen.* She made a remark about his sense of humor, since apparently he'd been suspected of running cocaine in your area for some time, but no one had ever been able to pin anything on him."

What did this have to do with Will shooting Benton and her being placed on leave? Deep inside, hope curled up like smoke.

"After MacPherson returned to Los Angeles to recover from her injuries, my narcotics team searched the *Snow Queen*. We found twenty kilos of high-grade cocaine concealed in a false ballast compartment in the hull."

Corelli dropped her pen, where it made the first mark on her clean notepad.

Joanna's mouth fell open. "*Twenty?* Just sitting there in the harbor with no guard, no nothing?"

Cooper smiled, and in that smile she saw the possibility of, if not a future, then at least the ability to wear her shield for one more afternoon.

"By that time, Richard Benton wasn't able to tell us how he might be involved with the cache, but Julian Royden was able to give us information about several people who used Bingham's sailboat. Mac-Pherson told us that he runs cocaine, but CLEU has never been able to gather enough evidence as to his methods. It turns out he has a triangular route between California, Oregon and Mexico, and he uses pleasure boats to transport the cargo. The *Snow Queen* is just one of them."

Holy crap. Proof at last.

Joanna tried to look calm and interested, as if her heart wasn't nearly leaping out of her chest. As if she wasn't dying to ask a million questions. As if she wasn't pathetically grateful to Cooper Maxwell for choosing this moment to reveal such a coup instead of quietly submitting it through the reporting system like any other investigator.

Cooper Maxwell isn't any other investigator. He's the guy who backed you up even when you didn't deserve it. Who was willing to step out on a limb and cut it out from under himself on the off chance you might be right. Who gambled big, risked everything—and for what?

For you.

Hope flickered up into the tiniest of flames.

"I would like to publicly thank Investigator Mac-Pherson—" how gracefully he gave her back her title "—for making the connection that led to the discovery of the cache. Because that's what has kept me in Santa Rita all this week," Cooper added. "Information came to light that a courier was going to take the sailboat into international waters and deliver it to a coastal town in Oregon. We were able to flip the courier so that when he delivered the kilos, we also got the Oregon arm of this distribution system. We've already made half a dozen arrests, including Mr. Anthony Bingham."

The breath went out of Joanna's lungs as she realized exactly why Cooper Maxwell hadn't called all week. He'd been busy taking down Anthony Bingham's organization, and giving her all the credit for cracking it.

If she didn't want to kiss him so bad, she'd just…well…cry.

"Congratulations, Investigators. Very well done." Martina Corelli looked up from the blot on her notepad, and picked up her pen once more. "Based on the testimony we've heard today, I would like to move that Investigator Joanna MacPherson be removed—"

Oh God, no!

"—from administrative leave and reinstated to her position with the Los Angeles Sub-Unit."

Joanna's throat backed up with tears of relief and gratitude that she absolutely must not shed.

"I also recommend that she be cleared of any culpability in the death of Richard Benton. I'm afraid her responsibility for the injuries to Anthony Bingham, Junior, aka 'Bling,' will stand on her record, but for the rest, I see no need for punitive action."

"Agreed," James Wilson said.

"Agreed," Ramirez echoed.

"This tribunal is ended at 12:10 hours," Corelli informed the tape recorder. "Investigators, you are free to go."

Cooper Maxwell held out his hand, and Joanna allowed him to pull her to her feet.

It was a good thing, too. Otherwise, she doubted her knees would have held her up.

22

"SO THIS IS where you hang your hat."

Cooper stood in the middle of the glossy hardwood floor and surveyed her TV and her couch, which were the only two things the living room contained.

Besides him. And damn, he looked good there.

"Thanks to you, I still have one to hang."

Beyond the sliding glass door, he looked out at her tiny section of grass. Some people planted flowers and shrubbery and hung things from their balconies. She was lucky the condo complex's groundskeeper watered the lawn. She barely had dishes to eat from. A garden hose and petunias were completely beyond her.

He shrugged out of his suit jacket and looked around for a place to put it.

"Here." There were hangers in the hall closet, at least. The jacket felt warm, and she resisted the temptation to bunch it between her hands and breathe in his scent. When he'd suggested debriefing somewhere off-site this afternoon, he'd been nothing but professional, and her invitation to come by the house had been nothing but cordial.

Well, maybe she hoped a little.

But to be on the safe side—in case his intentions were completely businesslike—she'd maintain an equally professional demeanor when all she wanted to do was drag him into the bedroom and kiss him until he couldn't breathe.

Essentially, she was right back to square one with him. Before the investigation had really kicked off, she'd thought those very same thoughts.

But things were different now, and frankly, she didn't have the guts to act the way she had then. Funny how the fear of losing what was most important to you could put everything in its place.

Just what is most important to you?

Her conscience was such a nag. She wished she could shut it off sometimes. But no, conscience or higher self or whatever the heck it was spoke up and editorialized whether she wanted it to or not.

Are you going to fight for him, girl, or go down whimpering?

Cooper turned from the window, and in his eyes she saw something she'd never seen before. Or maybe she had. The same expression had been on his face when she'd stumbled out of Benton's BMW and into his arms.

She wished she knew what it meant.

"I'm not taking any credit," he said. "It's their job to hassle us for our methods. It's our job to bring the bad guys in. They're not going to argue with success."

"Your success," she pointed out.

"Maybe, but it wouldn't have happened without you

making the connection." He paused. "I didn't come here to talk about work, Joanna."

Both of them still stood awkwardly in the middle of the room. Her home wasn't exactly…homey. Another thing she didn't have much of a gift for. Thank goodness she had a couch.

"Please." She gestured at it. "Sit down. Coffee?"

He shook his head and folded himself onto the couch, an arm extended along the back. She sat, too, a couple of inches out of reach of his fingers. That pose was inviting, but she wasn't in a position to trust body language at the moment.

"What did you come to talk about?"

His gaze flowed over her, warm as melted honey. "You and me."

That couldn't mean what she thought it meant. "The investigation is over, Cooper. You don't have to work with me anymore. We'll see each other in court, probably, over the next couple of years, but other than that…" Her voice trailed away.

"It's the *other than that* I want to talk about. Are you going to let me, or are you going to keep pretending I came here to debrief?"

"Didn't you?" she whispered. The flicker of hope she'd been sheltering inside herself flared up.

"Of course not. I came here so I could talk to you alone, without a whole office hearing about how I feel."

"Oh." Mentally, she rolled her eyes at herself. *Great, Joanna. Your eloquence is astounding.*

He reached over and pulled her into his arms. For a split second she considered maintaining her pride—and then abandoned it. What the hell.

Because this was where she belonged, crushed up against Cooper Maxwell's chest, feeling his heart beating under her ear, feeling his arms hard around her like he'd never let her go.

"That's better," he said with some satisfaction. Then his voice dropped until it was deep and husky. "You'll never know how I felt that moment when Benton pulled the knife and you keeled over. Will wasn't the only one who thought he'd used it on you. I swear my heart stopped beating completely."

"I never meant—I didn't know—"

His arms tightened around her in a quick squeeze. "It's pretty tough, you know, discovering that you love someone mere minutes before they take a knife and fall in the water. I can't think of anything that would clarify a guy's feelings more than that."

Whoa. Wait a minute. "Did you say…love?"

"Yeah, I did."

Her heart swelled with awe at the sheer bravery it took to say those words. "Love…me? Why?"

He grinned, and a deep dimple grooved one cheek. She figured she could spend the rest of her life looking at it and marveling that she could make him smile like that. "Who wouldn't love a gutsy, mouthy, leggy redhead who throws a mean kick and makes love like a goddess?"

"Well, if you put it that way." She snuggled into a comfy position with her cheek on his shoulder.

"How could you ask me that?" he murmured. "Why love you. What a question."

"I haven't given you many reasons to," she admitted. "I've done nothing but disobey orders and argue and get you into trouble."

"That's work. What about when we're alone? Think about that."

"Oh, that's even better. I turned you into a surrogate for my dad and disobeyed orders and argued and got you into trouble."

"The question is, do you still feel that way? Are we looking at a decade of therapy, here, or have things changed?"

She smiled, and breathed in the warm scent of him. Another thing she couldn't get enough of.

"You don't treat me the way he did. You treat me like a partner. An equal. Someone who has a brain and knows what to do. I couldn't handle it at first. I thought you were doing it to make a point or get something out of me. But then I realized…" She straightened so she could look into his eyes. "You were being sincere. And that's when things started to change." She paused. "And then when Benton told me the Rules are a bunch of bull and don't really work, I realized that was just an excuse, too. You know, that day on the sailboat. I wanted to make love to you, but I couldn't admit it to myself. So I made up this thing about using you for a test so I could let myself enjoy it."

"I'd have done it, test or not. I was crazy for you. Still am."

"I—" She took a deep breath. Her heart pounded, as if she stood on that dock again, looking down into the dark depths where danger and safety lay, combined. "I am, too. Crazy for you. Like I could stay here in your arms forever and not want one thing more."

"I could think of one thing."

"What?"

"I think we should test you again. You know. To make sure the Rules aren't affecting you any more."

"The Rules don't exist, silly." She nuzzled the strong line of his jaw, then worked her way up to his ear. "It's all in the guy's head. And in the girl's, too. I must be more suggestible than I ever thought. I still can't figure out how Thomas Semple managed it."

"Maybe they do exist," Cooper said. "Maybe we make up our own rules as we go."

She slid out of his arms and stood, holding out her hand. "Not for me. Rules of any kind are for the day job. When we're alone, I don't want any. I just want you and me and a bed."

He stood and took her hand. "I don't think we've ever made love on a bed."

"Now's the time to start." She led him toward the stairs. "Because I'll tell you, the bedroom is where I spend most of my time when I'm here."

He laughed, and anticipation made her pulse race and her steps pick up speed.

"Whatever else may change, I'll guarantee that's the one thing that won't."

She pulled him into her bright, sunny room and together, they made the leap onto her bed—and into their future.

* * * * *

THE ROYAL HOUSE OF NIROLI
Always passionate, always proud

The richest royal family in the world—united
by blood and passion, torn apart by deceit and desire

Nestled in the azure blue of the Mediterranean Sea, the
majestic island of Niroli has prospered for centuries.
The Fierezza men have worn the crown with passion
and pride since ancient times. But now, as the king's
health declines, and his two sons have been tragically
killed, the crown is in jeopardy.

The clock is ticking—a new heir must be found
before the king is forced to abdicate. By royal decree
the internationally scattered members of the Fierezza
family are summoned to claim their destiny. But any
person who takes the throne must do so according to
The Rules of the Royal House of Niroli. Soon secrets
and rivalries emerge as the descendant of this ancient
royal line vie for position and power. Only a true
Fierezza can become ruler—a person dedicated to their
country, their people…and their eternal love!

*Each month starting in July 2007, Harlequin Presents
is delighted to bring you an exciting installment from*
THE ROYAL HOUSE OF NIROLI,
*in which you can follow the epic search
for the true Nirolian king.
Eight heirs, eight romances, eight fantastic stories!*

Here's your chance to enjoy a sneak preview of the
first book delivered to you by royal decree…

FIVE minutes later she was standing immobile in front of the study's window, her original purpose of coming in forgotten, as she stared in shocked horror at the envelope she was holding. Waves of heat followed by icy chill surged through her body. She could hardly see the address now through her blurred vision, but the crest on its left-hand front corner stood out, its *royal* crest, followed by the address: *HRH Prince Marco of Niroli…*

She didn't hear Marco's key in the apartment door, she didn't even hear him calling out her name. Her shock was so great that nothing could penetrate it. It encased her in a kind of bubble, which only concentrated the torment of what she was suffering and branded it on her brain so that it could never be forgotten. It was only finally pierced by the sudden opening of the study door as Marco walked in.

"Welcome home, *Your Highness.* I suppose I ought to curtsy." She waited, praying that he would laugh and tell her that she had got it all wrong, that the envelope she was holding, addressing him as Prince Marco of Niroli, was some silly mistake. But like a tiny candle flame shivering vulnerably in the dark, her hope trembled fearfully. And then the look in Marco's eyes extinguished it as cruelly as a hand placed callously over a dying person's face to stem their last breath.

"Give that to me," he demanded, taking the envelope from her.

"It's too late, Marco," Emily told him brokenly. "I know the truth now…." She dug her teeth in her lower lip to try to force back her own pain.

"You had no right to go through my desk," Marco shot back at her furiously, full of loathing at being caught off guard and forced into a position in which he was in the wrong, making him determined to find something he could accuse Emily of. "I trusted you…."

Emily could hardly believe what she was hearing. "No, you didn't trust me, Marco, and you didn't trust me because you knew that I couldn't trust you. And you knew that because you're a liar, and liars don't trust people because they know that they themselves cannot be trusted." She not only felt sick, she also felt as though she could hardly breathe. "You are Prince Marco of Niroli…. How could you not tell me who you are and still live with me as intimately as we have lived together?" she demanded brokenly.

"Stop being so ridiculously dramatic," Marco demanded fiercely. "You are making too much of the situation."

"*Too much?*" Emily almost screamed the words at him. "When were you going to tell me, Marco? Perhaps you just planned to walk away without telling me anything? After all, what do my feelings matter to you?"

"Of course they matter." Marco stopped her sharply. "And it was in part to protect them, and you, that I decided not to inform you when my grandfather first announced that he intended to step down from the throne and hand it on to me."

"To protect me?" Emily nearly choked on her fury. "Hand on the throne? No wonder you told me when you first took me to bed that all you wanted was sex. You *knew* that was the only kind of relationship there could ever be between us! You *knew* that one day you would be Niroli's king. No doubt you are expected to marry a princess. Is she picked out for you already, your *royal* bride?"

* * * * *

*Look for THE FUTURE KING'S PREGNANT
MISTRESS
by Penny Jordan in July 2007,
from Harlequin Presents,
available wherever books are sold.*

HARLEQUIN®

Mediterranean NIGHTS™

Experience the glamour and elegance of cruising the
high seas with a new 12-book series....

MEDITERRANEAN NIGHTS

Coming in July 2007...

SCENT OF A WOMAN

by

Joanne Rock

When Danielle Chevalier is invited to an exclusive
conference aboard *Alexandra's Dream,* she knows it
will mean good things for her struggling fragrance
company. But her dreams get a setback when she
meets Adam Burns, a representative from a large
American conglomerate.

Danielle is charmed by the brusque American—
until she finds out he means to compete with her bid
for the opportunity that will save her family business!

www.eHarlequin.com

Silhouette

Desire

THE GARRISONS
A brand-new family saga begins with

THE CEO'S SCANDALOUS AFFAIR
BY ROXANNE ST. CLAIRE

Eldest son Parker Garrison is preoccupied running
his Miami hotel empire and dealing with his recently
deceased father's secret second family. Since he has
little time to date, taking his superefficient assistant
to a charity event should have been a simple plan.
Until passion takes them beyond business.

Don't miss any of the six exciting titles in
THE GARRISONS continuity, beginning in July.
Only from Silhouette Desire.

THE CEO'S SCANDALOUS AFFAIR
#1807

Available July 2007.

REQUEST YOUR FREE BOOKS!

2 FREE NOVELS PLUS 2 FREE GIFTS!

HARLEQUIN®

Blaze

Red-hot reads!

YES! Please send me 2 FREE Harlequin® Blaze® novels and my 2 FREE gifts. After receiving them, if I don't wish to receive any more books, I can return the shipping statement marked "cancel." If I don't cancel, I will receive 6 brand-new novels every month and be billed just $3.99 per book in the U.S., or $4.47 per book in Canada, plus 25¢ shipping and handling per book and applicable taxes, if any*. That's a savings of at least 15% off the cover price! I understand that accepting the 2 free books and gifts places me under no obligation to buy anything. I can always return a shipment and cancel at any time. Even if I never buy another book from Harlequin, the two free books and gifts are mine to keep forever.

151 HDN EF3W   351 HDN EF3X

Name	(PLEASE PRINT)
Address	Apt.
City	State/Prov.	Zip/Postal Code

Signature (if under 18, a parent or guardian must sign)

Mail to the **Harlequin Reader Service®:**
IN U.S.A.: P.O. Box 1867, Buffalo, NY 14240-1867
IN CANADA: P.O. Box 609, Fort Erie, Ontario L2A 5X3

Not valid to current Harlequin Blaze subscribers.

Want to try two free books from another line?
Call 1-800-873-8635 or visit www.morefreebooks.com.

* Terms and prices subject to change without notice. NY residents add applicable sales tax. Canadian residents will be charged applicable provincial taxes and GST. This offer is limited to one order per household. All orders subject to approval. Credit or debit balances in a customer's account(s) may be offset by any other outstanding balance owed by or to the customer. Please allow 4 to 6 weeks for delivery.

Your Privacy: Harlequin is committed to protecting your privacy. Our Privacy Policy is available online at www.eHarlequin.com or upon request from the Reader Service. From time to time we make our lists of customers available to reputable firms who may have a product or service of interest to you. If you would prefer we not share your name and address, please check here. ☐

HB07

Romantic
SUSPENSE

**Sparked by Danger,
Fueled by Passion.**

Mission: Impassioned

A brand-new miniseries begins with

My Spy

By *USA TODAY* bestselling author

Marie Ferrarella

She had to trust him with her life....
It was the most daring mission of Joshua Lazlo's
career: rescuing the prime minister of England's
daughter from a gang of cold-blooded kidnappers.
But nothing prepared the shadowy secret agent
for a fiery woman whose touch ignited something
far more dangerous.

My Spy

#1472

Available July 2007 wherever you buy books!

Visit Silhouette Books at www.eHarlequin.com   SRS27542

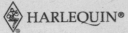

HARLEQUIN®

Blaze™

COMING NEXT MONTH

#333 MEN AT WORK Karen Kendall/Cindi Myers/Colleen Collins
Hot Summer Anthology
When these construction hotties pose for a charity calendar, more than a few pulses go through the roof! Add in Miami's steamy temperatures that beg a man to peel off his shirt and the result? Three sexy stories in one *very* hot collection. Don't miss it!

#334 THE ULTIMATE BITE Crystal Green
Extreme
A year ago he came to her—a vampire in need, seducing her with an incredible bite, an intimate bite…a forgettable bite? Haunted by the sensuality of that night, Kim's been searching for Stephen ever since. Imagine her surprise when she realizes he doesn't even remember her. And his surprise…when he discovers that Kim will do anything to become his Ultimate Bite…

#335 TAKEN Tori Carrington
The Bad Girls Club, Bk. 1
Seline Sanborn is a con artist. And power broker Ryder Blackwell is her handsome mark. An incredible one-night stand has Ryder falling, *hard*. But what will he do when he wakes up to find the angel in his bed gone…along with a chunk of his company's funds?

#336 THE COP Cara Summers
Tall, Dark…and Dangerously Hot! Bk. 2
Off-duty detective Nik Angelis is the first responder at a wedding-turned-murder-scene. The only witness is a fiery redhead who needs his protection—but *wants* his rock-hard body. Nik aims to be professional, but a man can take only so much….

#337 GHOSTS AND ROSES Kelley St. John
The Sexth Sense, Bk. 2
Gage Vicknair has been dreaming—incredible erotic visions—about a mysterious brown-eyed beauty. He's desperate to meet her and turn those dreams into reality. Only, he doesn't expect a ghost, a woman who was murdered, to be able to help him find her. Or that he's going to have to save the woman of his dreams from a similar fate….

#338 SHE DID A BAD, BAD THING Stephanie Bond
Million Dollar Secrets, Bk. 1
Mild-mannered makeup artist Jane Kurtz has always wished she had the nerve to go for things she wants. Like her neighbor Perry Brewer. So when she wins the lottery, she sees her chance—she's going to Vegas for the ultimate bad-girl makeover. Perry won't know what hit him. But he'll know soon. Because Perry's in Vegas, too….

www.eHarlequin.com